CW01209289

Wild Adventures in Time and Place

Denis O'Connor

authorHOUSE®

AuthorHouse™ UK Ltd.
1663 Liberty Drive
Bloomington, IN 47403 USA
www.authorhouse.co.uk
Phone: 0800.197.4150

© 2014 Denis O'Connor. All rights reserved.

No part of this book may be reproduced, stored in a retrieval system, or transmitted by any means without the written permission of the author.

Published by AuthorHouse 08/01/2014

ISBN: 978-1-4969-8692-4 (sc)
ISBN: 978-1-4969-8693-1 (e)

Any people depicted in stock imagery provided by Thinkstock are models, and such images are being used for illustrative purposes only.
Certain stock imagery © Thinkstock.

Because of the dynamic nature of the Internet, any web addresses or links contained in this book may have changed since publication and may no longer be valid. The views expressed in this work are solely those of the author and do not necessarily reflect the views of the publisher, and the publisher hereby disclaims any responsibility for them.

Contents

Slayco's War Party 1
The Wolf Research Agenda 62
An African Adventure 83
The Life of A National Serviceman 114
The Engagement 146
The Old Oak 168
The Legend of The Red Cat 177
The Parson's Kitten 205
The Wolf of Fuengirola 224

One night in the late sixties at a disco party with friends I was sitting having a drink while in somnolent mood when a day dream played a story through my mind. I determined that someday I would write it down and so, many years later, here it is.

Slayco's War Party

THE AMBUSH

Desperately they rode out of the night into the dusty yellow of a Mojave Desert dawn, a man and a boy double mounted on a tough Morgan horse. On the wild and lonesome trail from Sante Fe overland to the gold boom towns of the developing West Coast, they were now running badly short of water and food. Five days back after fording the low water reaches of the Rio Grande where it half circled Fort Apache they had taken on provisions that they had expected to last them until they reached Phoenix to the West. From there it would be just a short haul to Salome and then on to Yuma from whence they could cross the Colorado and head North into sweet water mountain country and buy a few acres for grazing cattle, build a homestead and live off the land.

Four days out on the trail they'd spotted a column of black smoke on the horizon. Not long afterwards they came across a bunch of distressed survivors of a wagon train that had been attacked by Commanches intent on a hate raid to rape and plunder. The fifteen men, eight women and six children had lost everything they owned except the horses they were riding. Even so they reckoned themselves fortunate to have escaped with their lives from the hell of burning wagons and the bloody slaughter of their fellow travellers. They were running scared and paused only to give a warning about rampaging painted demons who attacked silently out of a black moonless night. The survivors of the wagon train were heading hot foot for Silver City to the East and urged the man with the boy to join them. But thanking them kindly and sharing some of his coffee and dried beans with them he wished the party good luck as they sped off. Meanwhile he and the boy swung North by North West and headed at a fast lick into desert country hoping to skirt any dangers that might be lurking nearby and make up for lost time. But the Mojave Desert is a wild forbidding place full of unexpected dangers and sudden changes of weather can take a traveller by surprise no matter how well prepared. Fiercely hot by day and freezing cold by night it is not a region for any but the stout hearted who are accustomed and equipped to endure hardship.

Suffering the privations of the raw night chill as they travelled along their way they were anxious for a rest come daybreak but as they searched for a place to camp they became lost during a blinding sandstorm which forced them to stop and take cover for several hours. Afterwards they had to make a wide detour to avoid further dust clouds streaming across the horizon which cost them several days extra ride and depleted their already meagre provisions. It was bad luck that a roaming Chiricahua Apache war party struck their trail just about nightfall on their third day in desert country. The war party, a band of young braves led by a renegade war chief called Yellow Snake, were more than eager to count coup and do some killing to confirm their warrior status.

Their eagerness to give chase was aroused by the deep tracks of a shod horse in the sandy desert scrub. The signs excited their bloodlust at the prospect of capturing a white man with a horse, guns and food. And even more, if they took him alive, the slow torture and death of the white would charge them with spirit power.

Lost in the wilderness around them, the man listened anxiously to the sounds carried on the rising desert wind and the startling call of a prairie owl that wasn't a prairie owl. Intuitively he felt the presence of danger close at hand. Three years of tough fighting in the Civil War between the N orth and the South had honed his soldiering senses to a sharp edge. They would serve him well now. Cautiously he pushed a trail through the scattered scrub changing direction with practised ease as, glancing fearfully from side to side, he rode nearer to a cluster of high standing rocks arising out of the sandy terrain. Every moment brought the massive pillars of rock nearer and he could now just see the first red glow of the rising sun touching the tops of the rocky outcrops. Hope began to rise within him as he drew closer. If he could reach the huge boulders ahead there would be a chance, maybe a slim chance of making a stand against whoever was trailing him.

When the ambush came there was no time to think only to react. Apaches do not attack on horseback as Commanches do. They ride to where they intend to fight and then dismount to join battle on foot. Somehow they had got ahead of him and were lying in wait. One second the man seemed alone in a wild and darkened landscape and the next he was galloping flat out and fighting for their lives. The brown dusky bodies of squat barrel chested men rose silently from ground that seemed to offer no cover. Incredibly swift, slashing and lunging with knife and lance, the Apaches tried to bring down the horse first. Rising from the saddle and letting the reins drop loose, the man grabbed the new Spencer Rifle from the scabbard and blasted at point blank range into the hideously painted face of a brave about to cut the Morgan's throat. Without hesitation he swung the rifle around to cover his left flank and fired two quick shots at the savages closing in from that side. One of the savages stumbled at the impact of the heavy calibre slug and, although wounded, still managed to fling his tomahawk, just missing the rider but gouging a wound in the horse's hindquarters. Squealing with pain and shock the horse bolted and swerved straight into the path of a young Apache brave about to count coup. Knocked of his feet the warrior was torn apart by pounding steel hooves as the horse and rider fled for the shelter of the rocks ahead. The rider's quick action and the speed of his mount afforded them a brief respite from the attack and soon they reached the protection of the huge crags. Behind them three lay dead along the trail and another held his side as he limped away. But the rest, moving silently on moccasined clad feet and hidden by the early morning shadows within the ravines, swung doggedly in pursuit, the battle hardened amongst them determined more than ever now to make a kill.

Dismounting swiftly in the shelter of the rocks, the man stripped the blanket from his six year old son and lifted him down from the saddle where he'd crouched during the hectic ride. He knew that he had little time before the Indians would close on him but he spoke gently to the lad as they drank water together from the canteen and ate some beef jerky. Then hoisting the boy on his shoulders he pushed him up the face of a smooth slab of rock all the while murmuring soft words of endearment and encouragement. Lastly he commanded the boy to stay hidden no matter what happened or what he might hear and tossed him a water canteen with a Bowie Knife strapped around it. Then he gave a final wave of farewell as his son disappeared high up amongst the rocks.

Retracing his steps he took up the blanket that had covered the boy and with it wiped away his tracks in the soft sand to where he'd hidden his son. Then he unsaddled his horse and poured water from his spare canteen into his cavalry hat for the exhausted animal to drink. Afterwards he slipped off the bridle and turned the animal loose. Working with feverish anxiety he now turned his attention to his guns. Selecting a long table top rock that afforded him sight of the desert expanse in front yet enclosed him from the back and sides he knew he'd found the best defensive position. Here he would make his stand.

He possessed a considerable armoury. There was a pair of Colt Army percussion revolvers, one of which he wore in a holster attached to his belt the other he kept in the saddle bag along with a .44 Dragoon Colt of 1847 vintage. Then there was a Spencer Rifle, special edition model which had been presented to him as an award for exceptional valour and which bore his name and rank engraved on a silver plaquie bolted to the rifle butt. There were two cartridge tubes, each containg seven cartridges for the rifle. He checked all the guns for ammunition and, laying them out on the rock in front of him, he covered them with the blanket to protect them from the heat of the sun. One of the Colts he loaded fully and kept in the holster on his right hand side the other he slid under the edge of the blanket close to his left hand. As ready as he could be he sat in the shadows with the spare canteen at his side awaiting the attack. He guessed the Apaches would wait until the sun was high enough to cause the heated desert ground to shimmer and afford them some cover for the assault against him. Meanwhile his thoughts turned to his six year old boy, a fine son, who embodied all his hopes for the future. When he had returned from the war he found that his wife had died and the boy was being cared for by neighbours. Deciding to make a clean start in the West he'd bought a horse for the boy and a mule to backpack some belongings and provisions, the Morgan was already a trusted mount which had accompanied him faithfully for the duration of the war. A prolonged spell of bad weather culminating in a fierce storm had thrown him off track and the mule had been lost. Not long after the boy's horse had gone lame and had to be set loose. Thereafter he had ridden double mounted with the boy's wiry frame tucked in front of him and the hope that they'd find a town where he could buy another horse and replenish his supplies. But he'd reckoned without the desert and its wild moods, they'd become lost and then came his worst nightmare as they were stalked by a band of Apaches. He reflected bitterly that the luck which had seen him safely through over four years of bloody and brutal warfare had now turned and unless a miracle happened he was doomed to die. He bitterly regretted having to abandon his son and it seared him emotionally to think what little hope there was for the boy's survival. Well, the Indians would rush him soon and he was determined to kill as many as he could before they got him. He was outnumbered and he knew from harsh experience he faced an enemy who would show him no quarter. His one remaining hope was that his son would somehow survive. He had heard stories that Apaches sometimes took captured male children to rear as their own but he suspected that this war band was after blood.

"Why were they waiting?" he wondered and then he realised that the sun was moving around the sky to a point where, about noon, it would be shining directly in his face. So they would attack at noon when the desert heat had sucked the energy out of him and when the heat waves from the desert would screen their assault. Nervously he wiped the sweat from his face and strained to see what was happening out there. On the flat scrubland before him he could spot nothing except an occasional dust flurry. His heart thumped and his hands began to sweat but not just because of the heat which was bad enough but due to being on a raw edge. It he had always been like that just before a battle during the War. He thought of home and the wife he'd had. And then his thoughts turned to the home he had intended to make with his boy.

He'd have wanted to build a sturdy log cabin in a plot of verdant land. Then he would dig a well to serve the ranch house, grow a few crops to store as food and buy some livestock for milk and beef. He'd reckoned they could have made a good life for themselves given the chance but now that chance was gone and with it the hope for a fulfilling future. His savings, with his army pay and the little he'd accumulated from the sale of his former homestead, was in the money belt he'd buckled around his son's waist. If the boy survived the money could be put to good use. As these thoughts tumbled around his mind he became aware of a slight movement on his right flank. Swiftly drawing his Army Colt he whirled around to face the intruder only to find it was his faithful Morgan come back to be with him. This horse was special in every way and it was typical of it to seek out his company now. The wound on its rump was bleeding from the tomahawk wound and he did his best to stop the flow and seal it with gun powder from one of his bullets which he prised open with his sheath knife. The horse nuzzled him affectionately and he stroked the strong brown neck and flanks. He wished he could save this magnificent animal from death or at least capture by the Indians but it refused to leave him. He led it into the shade of some tall boulders. There was just a slim chance that he could kill them all since it was only a small war party as far as he could tell but he'd have to wait and see what happened. As the desert and the rocks around him heated up there was no respite from the sun's furnace. It was just about noon he reckoned and they'd be coming soon. He wiped away the sweat running down his face and blinding his eyes, drank a little from his canteen and sought to focus on the desert shimmering in the unrelenting heat. Suddenly they were out there in front of him before he had time to sense the onset of the attack. They stormed across the scrub and sandy plain towards him, dust covered bodies stooped low to the ground surging forward like a wolf pack, ghostly figures presenting indistinct targets in the filmy haze. The first arrow hit him high in the right shoulder, the shock causing him to drop his sixgun unfired. He shot off all the chambers in the colt held in his left hand and then they were on him. They impaled him with short war stabbing lances, smashed his head in with tomahawk blows and cut out his heart with quick knife thrusts. It was over before he had time to reach for any of his other guns and by then he was already dead from multiple wounds. High above the Indians ravaging his father's body, a little boy, from a concealed rock crevice, watched unseen with the sun behind him. With tears streaming down his face and racked by an agony of torment his ears were assailed by the shrill war cries of triumph, sounds like 'Slayco' repeated over and over again by the savages. The sound imprinted itself on his mind and would be remembered all his life. He also would never forget the face of the Indian leader wearing the yellow headband, the one who triumphantly grabbed his father's rifle and who would become notorious throughout the region as the war chief Yellow Snake. He could watch no more and slumped back against his rock hideaway swooning into a faint. Mercifully he missed the sight of the Apaches feasting on some of his father's flesh, the heart and other organs, which they cooked over a slow fire and shared with each other to absorb the power of the hated white man. Then they rode off with the guns, the blanket and the Morgan horse; they left the saddle and saddle bags as useless baggage.

RESCUE

Several miles to the East on the trail from Tucson three riders crossed the Morgan's trail. Dan Blue Feather, the Cheyenne Indian half breed, dismounted and ran his hand and fingers over the deep imprints of an iron shod horse. From a kneeling position he raised his head and addressed the others. "Kinda looks like somebody's carrying a pack of gold or something." A tall thickset man named Jenson, a former Texas Ranger, looked over at the tracks without dismounting. "What do you think Kid" he turned to a lean young man astride an Appaloosa. "Could be worth a look-see" came the answer from the young man variously known as the Wichita Kid but who bore the name Jed Henry after a grandfather who'd died at the Alamo. "Well let's get to it" Jenson said. "Dan you pick out his trail." And with that they rode off in line Indian style. Pretty soon the Breed halted once more, "Looks like he got company." He rode a way ahead and began circling and reading sign. Riding back to join the others he reported what to him was bad news. "Seems like he was being tailed by a wild bunch riding Apache war ponies. They hid the ponies over there and ambushed him on foot but they took more trouble than they reckoned. Three dead and mebbe some wounded. They then followed his trail towards them rocks. Looks like bad medicine." Jenson glanced appreciatively at Dan. Usually the Breed said very little but that was quite a speech. He never ceased to wonder at the skills of this man who was his friend and who couldn't read a word in a book but as a tracker could not be bettered. He turned to the Kid saying "We could be riding ourselves into a heap of trouble if we keep on following this trail." The Kid grinned broadly "So when did a little trouble bother you?" "Ever since I started riding with you two and I ain't figuring on riding slap bang into an Apache ambush." "Mebbe so mebbe's not but ahh reckon we could take the chance and come out rich." Jenson frowned "What do you think Dan?" The half breed stared towards the rock pillars that stood out red in the afternoon sun without answering. "Hell, let's do it!" At Jenson's words they all paused, feeling the excitement pulsing through them at the prospect of danger ahead. Holding their horses they checked their guns in case it came to a shoot out. It could mean the difference between the quick and the dead. Satisfied at last they moved ahead, each one of them alert for the least sign that might spell sudden death. The sky was beginning to darken and what had minutes ago been a light wind was now gathering up a storm. Their horses stomped along uneasy at the change in the weather, jerking nervously as clumps of tumbleweed rolled past them. The men, veterans of desert travelling, knew there'd soon be one hell of a sandstorm brewing up and they needed to find shelter excepting that the only shelter available could be hiding a pack of trouble like a parcel of killer Indians lying in wait. Jenson unsheathed his scatter gun with the sawn off barrel. The other two also drew weapons. Dismounting each man led his horse with one hand and in the other cradled a gun ready for action. It was Dan, the half-breed, who first sensed that something wasn't right and raised a hand to alert the others. A light avalanche of small rocks and stones caused each of the men to hit the ground fast. "There's someone up there" barked Jenson raising his gun as he caught sight of a shadow moving high up in the crags. But it was Dan Blue Feather again who saw that there wasn't really a problem "Don't shoot, it's only a kid" he shouted in warning as the distraught figure of a child stumbled forwards atop a huge slab of rock. The Wichita Kid ran towards the foot of the stone pillar where the boy crouched. The Kid, always one with an easy smiling style for folks, especially children and women, now talked the soft spoken words that brought the six year old sliding down safely into his arms. "Looks like we've got ourselves a live one" Jenson said. "What's your name boy?" At first the child couldn't or wouldn't speak. Meanwhile Dan Blue Feather had made a quick reconnaissance of the area and now, looking sort of spooked, he spoke in rapid half whispers to Jenson who nodded and advised the Wichita Kid to take the boy over to where the horses were standing and give him something to drink. "He might like one of those dough biscuits we saved from breakfast this morning" he volunteered. Then he and

Danny walked over to a sprawl of rocks where a fire had been lit and there were bones and some burnt flesh which were the only remains of the man who'd fought the Apaches. Looks like they had themselves quite a party. Didn't know that Apaches did some cannablising like I heard Crows and Utes do." "Sometimes" the Breed grunted" For the Power." "Well, let's get this mess buried before the boy sees it." Meanwhile the Wichita Kid had managed to find out the boy's first name. Later when the other two joined him he told them what he'd learned. "He's called Ben but as for the rest he just keeps mouthing 'Slayco' or something sounding like that. Is that Indian lingo?" he asked Dan. The Breed only shook his head and grimaced. Dan had read the ground sign and indicated that the Apaches had left on a heading South. "Probably got a camp where they can hole up in the Mexican Sierras. Let's get outa here before any more turn up. Kid you got the best horse; take the boy." And with that they high tailed it for Phoenix, riding abreast through the gathering storm so they wouldn't be eating each other's dust. Ben Slayco, as he was now to be known, huddled against the Wichita Kid as they rode along at a steady pace, still too shocked to come to terms with what he had seen. The death of his father, his only family, preyed heavy on his mind. Jenson had in mind to rendezvous at the U.S. Cavalry Camp at Fort Commanche just outside Phoenix. He knew the Commanding Officer there Colonel Charles Shennigan for whom he'd done some scouting and Indian

Wild Adventures in Time and Place

hunting along with Dan Blue Feather. The Colonel would know what to do with this orphan white boy.

It took some hard riding to find the trail north to Phoenix. Many times they dismounted and hid to avoid what they took to be roaming bands of Commanches on the warpath. This perplexed Jenson because Dan had identified Apache sign back at the big rock formation where they'd found the boy. So it was near dark when they reached Fort Commanche which was an army type stockade built of wood with adobe walls to protect the inhabitants of Phoenix and the wagon trains moving west from marauding Indians and Mexican Bandits. Jenson hailed the guard and the gates were opened. Apart from the guard patrols the Fort was settled down for the night. They managed to rustle up some grub from the cookhouse but the boy wouldn't eat anything. The Sergeant of the Guard found them a place to bed down and Jenson arranged through him to see the Colonel come morning. During the night they were awakened by the sounds of gunfire when a group of settlers' wagons were attacked near the Fort and a Cavalry Patrol, sent to their aid, fought a bloody skirmish with Commancheros who were on the rampage for weapons, women and provisions. It was the year 1866 and the Western territories were still in ferment following the mayhem of the Civil War. As one old army veteran put it "Who said the War is over?" The truth of his words could be found everywhere along the lawless boom towns fringing the Rio Grande where the killing, looting and raping went ahead unabated by the declarations of peace from Washington in the North to Atlanta in the South.

The next morning Jenson met with Colonel Charles Shennigan and apprised him of the situation. "You say the boy is quite young." "Yes Sir, no more than five or six years old but he's had shock. It looks like the man he was with, mebbe's a father or brother, hid him up in the rocks before being killed by Apaches. Leastways that's how it looks."

"Does the boy have a name?" "All we could get from him was the name Ben and then some sort of savage or Mexican lingo sounding like 'Slayco."

The Colonel said nothing for a while but stood at the window overlooking the parade ground. Jenson's account had stirred a notion in his mind that would need some further thought after he'd spoken to Martha, his wife. He turned to the big man standing by his desk. "Where is this boy now?" he asked. "Well Sir he's sort of hunkered down and having some breakfast with Dan Blue Feather and the Wichita Kid. The Kid's kinda taken to the boy and is trying to get some food into him." Jenson paused, unused to making long speeches, he began fiddling with his hat. He just wanted the Colonel to make a decision so he could get out of there and continue the planned journey to Silver City.

"Have the boy brought to my quarters. I must go and have a word with my wife." And with that, to Jenson's immense relief, the meeting was over. The Colonel reached the wooden army shack that he and his wife were to treat temporarily as their home. Martha was surprised to see him so early again and exclaimed "Why Charles is anything wrong?" At that moment Jenson arrived with the boy and her eyes widened with surprise. "Let's all go inside Col. Shennigan" said and by way of explanation to his startled wife he added "Martha, I'd like you to hear Major Jenson's tale about how he came by this boy." The term 'Major' was a courtesy to Jenson who had been forced to retire from the Cavalry after being badly wounded in the Battle at Bull Run. In the cosily furnished parlour they all sat and talked and the talk was mainly to do with what was to be done with the boy known only as Ben Slayco. He sat quietly as Jenson once more related the details of finding him. At last the big man was free to leave the house, a man of the plains and wide open spaces he felt uncomfortable and claustrophobic when surrounded by walls and a roof overhead. He turned to the boy and simply said "Here's wishing you luck, Ben. You're in good hands now." Ben watched his saviour go without saying anything. He was still back there in the desert hearing the eerie cries that would forever haunt his mind. He felt numbed and frightened and his uncertain future was now in the hands of strangers. The outcome was that the Shennigans, unable to have children of their own, would take the boy and bring him up as theirs. The Colonel was due to retire in another few years and they would be moving back East where his wife's wealthy family had business and political connections. For Ben Slayco, life with his new found family would offer the security he had never known. Yet there was still the thought deep in his mind of taking revenge against the Apaches, especially the war chief who wore the yellow band around his forehead and who had taken his beloved father away from him. Some day that thought would emerge into action, there was no doubt about that.

PART II
MANHOOD

Ben 'Slayco' Shennigan lived a secure and happy young life as the adopted but beloved son of Charles and Martha Shennigan. Whilst the Colonel eked out the rest of his military career on the frontier Ben was given the run of the Fort. He learned to ride and shoot as good as any trooper and better than most before he was but fourteen years old due to the efforts of the company of battle hardened men who delighted in teaching him their skills.

He grew to love the stretches of desert near his home at the Fort. The Shennigans encouraged him to explore the area always observing due caution. Martha, daughter of a genteel family, sought to cultivate an awareness in Ben of the finer things in life and with this purpose in mind she read poetry and selections of literature to him. She attempted to lighten his dark moods with songs she sang to him and Ben grew to love her and the culture she embodied. But at heart the boy was an enigma even to himself. The Shennigans seemed to acknowledge that there was more than a trace of wildness in the boy that needed fostering. He learned the basics of reading and writing from the rough schoolhouse adjoining the Chapel situated within the Army's enclosure. The Minister's wife did the schooling most mornings of the week and Ben's afternoons were spent either hanging around some of the Apache scouts, who talked endlessly of by-gone times, or riding out alone. He didn't mix much with the few other kids as if he had time only for the things going on in his own head. Central to his interests was coming to terms with the wilderness around him as he struggled to understand the ways of the Indian tribes, the Kiowas, the Apaches and especially the Commanches who posed an ever present threat to the lives of the soldiers and the settlers.

He loved to savour the unique appeal of the light on the desert scrubland as it changed the scenic aura of the moment. In the soft light of early dawn the colours of the sky touched the ravines and dry gulches with blushing tints of pink and gold radiant in the clear pure air. Around noon the heat of the sun turned the terrain into a seething furnace that sent the coyotes, gophers, jack rabbits and even the snakes scuttling to earth for cover. With the heat would come the winds stirring up the ground into blinding dust storms that fanned the heat into flames consuming mesquite, tumble weed and dry grasses in flash fires that soon petered out. The Commanche called them Spirit Fire which marked the presence of their ancestors riding the plains on fire horses. But the evenings could bring the best mood swing of all when the land was tired of agitation and just lay down to rest. Smokey hazes clouded the horizon and the brown earth was streaked with charred black striations that picked out the shallow furrows beneath the ridged surfaces where quail and sage hens roosted in the hollows. Ben favoured the gentle half light of evening time when the sky was a blaze with orange hues and delicate bands of colour like desert flowers blooming after rain. With the onset of night would come the cold, coldness that could suck the heat out of a man and leave him as frozen as a block of ice.The desert underwent mood changes that defied the understanding just like the red skinned men who rode its trails and called it theirs and in whom it bred an extreme form of savagery.

For the white homesteaders the end of day was a time of peace and restfulness but it could also bring a fearful dread of the coming night when Indian war parties attacked in murderous raids. Despite the presence of a few cavalry units the Army was unable to keep the peace and the frontier country was descending into tumult. For thousands of years it had belonged to the Indians. But now a race of white skinned folk were taking over the land. They were farmers, ranchers and settlers wanting to make homes to raise families, build schools and churches where formerly there was only wilderness. The Indian tribes had developed a way of living that was in tune with the natural landscape but this way of life brought them into direct conflict with the 'civilised' ways of the white people. War was inevitable even though there were those men of good faith from each side who attempted to achieve a peaceful compromise. This was the world in which Ben Slayco grew up and imbibed the lore of the wild western frontier.

The Shennigans gave him the loving support he needed and at the age of twenty one he graduated with honours from West Point Military Officer Training Establishment. His adoptive parents were singularly proud of him no more than if he had been their own flesh and blood. They tried to ensure through their contacts in Washington that he would be posted to one of the more prestigious army command units in the East but despite their best intentions for his career Ben requested a posting far to the South where the army was obliged to maintain a presence in what still remained unsettled country where hostile bands of Indians and bandits continued to roam freely. To this end he was posted to Fort Sumner in the New Mexico Territories. It did not escape his mind that perhaps fate would extend him the chance to settle an old score with an Apache War Chief who carried his father's rifle and who had progressed to become one of the most murderous Apaches since Geranimo. As such he ranked high on the U.S. Cavalry's most wanted list, to be taken dead or alive, which suited Ben 'Slayco' Shennigan just fine.

YELLOW SNAKE

The Apache who was to be the focus of Ben's thirst for revenge had his origins in the early years of the 1850's under the protective shadow of the North Mexican Sierras where the Athapaskan- Apache People had long found safety and refuge in the numerous mountain caves. He was born to a War Chief and his squaw just as the morning sun broke the sky into shards of gold and crimson. The baby's given Indian name translated as 'Yellow Cloud at Dawnlight' and during his boyhood and teenage years he was known as Yellow Cloud. At the time of puberty in accordance with the custom of the tribe he was sent alone into the hills with a supply of water and a rawhide pouch containing a concoction of dried herbs and resins from tree bark prepared by the tribal Medicine Man. This was all he was allowed to eat to induce a trance state wherein he would be imbued with the wisdom of his ancestors who would approach him in animal form, such as an eagle or a wolf, and convey to him wisdom through their 'Spirit Talk.' Alone with only the winds from high mountain places for company his mind would be cleansed and refreshed. At the end of this period of initiation into adulthood as he made his way down a deep narrow gorge he was attacked and bitten by a snake, the one Apaches called 'Yellow Snake' and white men dub 'Rattle Snake.' The snake bit him in the arm as he descended. Taken by surprise he nevertheless was able to grab the reptile by the tail and whiplashed its head against a rock killing it immediately. Unable to reach the bite to suck out the venom, the poison circulated throughout his body and caused him to lose consciousness. He lay comatose as his body fought the deadly toxins. Since he failed to return after the expected time of absence his father sent a search party to find him. When they first came across his body they thought that he was dead but on returning with him to the village the shaman, Moon Wolf, detected a heartbeat and ordered him to be wrapped in a buffalo robe and laid in a dark tepee. At night the village performed a Medicine Dance for his recovery with much clamour, singing and shrieking and in the evening of the day following Yellow Cloud regained consciousness but he was changed. During the period of what the Indians called his 'Death Sleep,' spirit dreams had shown him a future in which he would take a bloody revenge for the suffering his people had endured especially from the whites who had invaded their land and desecrated their holy places. The snake had only been the agent of his new awakening and henceforth he would take its name and wear its yellow skin for a headband. The tribe were amazed at the change in one so young but respected the spirit medicine that now possessed him. In closed consultation with the shaman the signs were read and it became clear that he must leave the village and his tribe and go on the war path alone. Others would join him as he built up his power. Soon the his new name Yellow Snake would become revered among the Apaches and mortally feared amongst white settlers and even among bands of the Commanche, traditional enemies of the Apache people.

Away from the tribe he had time to think, to work out a strategy that would give him a direction for the rest of his life, He knew that to survive against the odds stacked against him he would need to totally embrace the ways of the warrior. He would need to follow the path of the dark spirits, to be guided by their ways. He thought of how the Commanche surpassed even the Apaches for cruelty and acts of torture and how their deadly attacks had driven his people North beyond their natural hunting grounds and settlements where they had encountered new conflicts with the encroaching white people. So now he must adopt the code of the wolf and pursue relentlessly with savagery and lethal intent those who were his enemy. Born of the tough Chiricahua mountain people whose braves could run and walk over fifty miles a day and then mount a raid and who included amongst their leaders the great warrior chief Cochise and also the rogue desperado Geronimo, Yellow Snake would exceed all that had previously passed for warrior prowess in cunning and savagery. In this time of adversity he needed to take up the mantle of the foe and become more Commanche for ferocity and malice than the Commanche themselves. He would outdo them all in malevolence and he would defeat who ever and whatever came against him or die in the combat. Meanwhile he had this urgent need to accrue power.

∽

AN OLD FRIEND

Lieutenant Ben Shennigan soon became fully acquainted with a cavalry soldier's life on the wild western frontier. Each day brought fresh incidents of disorder and havoc requiring intervention by the Army. As the newest officer recruit to the limited force at Fort Sumner, Ben found himself rapidly absorbed into the frequent engagements dealing with Indian attacks and lawless turmoil in the border towns caused by shootings between drunken cowboys and fracases among itinerant gamblers. As his experience widened he noticed a recognisable pattern to the more bloody and barbaric attacks by the Apache led war bands. On patrol one day his small cavalry unit came upon the latest atrocity. The stage to Tucson had been attacked and wrecked. The passengers and crew massacred, the luggage ransacked and the six horse team taken. As Ben dismounted to survey the outrage

Sergeant Drummond, a veteran of many such patrols, called out to him

"You'd best come and look see here, Lieutenant."

Ben strolled over to where several troopers were untying a body that had been hung upside down from a giant cactus. One of the troopers broke away from the detail to vomit and the others wore pale and pained expressions as they lowered the mutilated body to the ground. Sgt. Drummond faced Ben saying:

"He's barely alive Sir. What should we do?"

Ben moved closer to the man's body which had been laid out on the ground and which had a strangely familiar look to it. As he got closer the ghastly realisation struck him that he knew this man and then he recalled a smiling gentle voiced gunman who had shared his horse with a boy and had coaxed him to eat in those first frantic days after he was rescued so many years ago. The mangled and tortured body belonged to the Witchita Kid or what was left of him. The savages had tied him upside down from a cactus tree, slit his belly and his genitals and lit a fire about a foot under his head. Suddenly the eyes opened in the burnt just recognisable face and the lips parted as if he was trying to say something. Ben, in an agony of torment, stared desperately at the friend from his past. He realised suddenly what the Kid wanted him to do.

"Shall I do the necessary, Sir. We can't leave him suffering can we?"

"No Sergeant. I once knew this man. It's my call."

And with that Ben drew his service revolver and fired two killing shots into the dying man. Then in a shocked daze, as the troopers dug graves for the bodies, he walked around the site of the massacre to ascertain what to put in his report. It was likely, he thought, that the Wichita Kid had been riding 'Shot Gun Guard' for the stage driver and had survived the crash when the stage overturned. All the other men, six in all including the driver, had been shot outright. A woman, mebbe in her thirties, had been raped and mutilated in death. It seems that the Kid had been taken alive because, an expert shot, he'd probably gunned down some of the raiding party. Although the Apaches knew help would be sent when the stage didn't show in town, they'd taken the time to torture him. The arrival of Ben's Patrol had chased them off before they'd been able to 'Take Power' from his slow death. The patrol army guide, a Pawnee, had read the sign around the stage as belonging to Apache Ponies most likely from Yellow Snake's warriors he announced. As Ben watched his troopers burying the bodies he reflected on what he'd known about the Wichita Kid chiefly from what Jenson had told him. The Kid's life had been spent mainly in the boom towns along the Rio Grande but of his origins nothing was known. In his short adult life he had ridden with some of the infamous guerrilla outlaw groups during the Civil War but afterwards had followed a mottled career as a some-time hired gun, a town marshal and a pony express rider. Ben remembered him mainly as a kindly, smiling man who'd charmed a frightened little boy down from his hideout among the rocky crags above where his father had been killed. And now the Kid was gone, murdered by probably the same Indian responsible for his father's death. With a heavy heart Ben ordered his troop back to the Fort. Now he had yet another 'Payback' that this hated Apache owed to him.

THE NIGHT THEY BURNED PHOENIX

After several days of routine duties there was a new development. There had been a serious breakout at the San Carlos Indian Reservation. All the young braves and even the resident Apache Reservation Police had left due to the abiding frustration with bad food and boredom and it was rumoured they were to join up with Yellow Snake. The gossip talk among the 'old tame' Indians living around the Fort was that something big was about to happen although it was not clear how they knew. Four days later Fort Commanche was attacked and burned down by an Apache force under Yellow Snake's command. The Indians waited until late afternoon when the last patrol had returned then they crashed two freight wagons they'd stolen earlier laden with barrels of coal oil into the stockade and set fire to them. In the raging fire that ensued, the Fort defences were breached and overwhelmed with serious casualties. At about the same time a main force, led by Yellow Snake himself, launched a ferocious raid on Phoenix City and the environs where several settler wagon trains were resting. A cavalry trooper, wounded in the attack, brought the news of the assault to Fort Sumner. He reported that the Apache Chief know s Yellow Snake had been identified as the Indian leader who had led the attack. A relief column was immediately dispatched to the scene. Ben's patrol was one of the first to reach the outskirts of the city. The fire from burning buildings and wagons could be seen from miles away and the stench of burning bodies was carried on the wind. As they drew nearer the screams of the victims could be heard over the rattle of gunfire and the war cries of the rampaging Apaches. Ben's troop immediately drew sabres and charged some Indians who were plundering a store house. Once he rode into what was left of the city Ben realised how devastating the raid had been. Taken totally by surprise the town's people had put up a token defence but the evidence of wholesale carnage was everywhere with the bodies of the dead and dying lying all around. As Ben's patrol advanced the Apaches vanished and apart from firing at the few remaining looters his troop saw little action. Soon the remains of the city were under the control of the army and the roundup of the survivors was in hand. One building, the formidable Town Hall which was built of stone and hardwood, had survived the attack and the fire raising and had served as a redoubt for some of the town's menfolk who had armed themselves with rifles and fought off repeated Indian attacks.

High on a bluff overlooking the devastation he had caused, Yellow Snake led his band towards their hideout among the ragged rocks and canyons. His warriors had plundered a plentiful supply of provisions to support his campaign. A line of weeping women hostages, hands bound and lashed together, were pulled along barefoot over the stony ground. They would be summarily raped and then bartered with the Commancheros for weapons and ammunition. Yellow Snake paused, standing tall for an Apache, and looking back he snarled his defiance at the enemy he felt destined to destroy

With the advent of morning tempers flared in the groups of survivors and harsh words were spoken about the lack of military defence against the growing Indian problem since the Texas Rangers had been disbanded. Many of the former residents were leaving in droves, shocked and distressed at the unthinkable happenings of the previous night. They were nevertheless relieved to be alive.

SLASHER STONE

News of the City's demise and the atrocities committed by the Apaches reached Washington and caused outrage in the Federal Government. President Grover Cleveland ordered an immediate solution to this crisis and commissioned one, Colonel Bruce Stone, a hardline right wing republican career officer, to lead a major force against the savages "Out there in the West."

Slasher Stone, as the Colonel was popularly known, had made a name for himself at WestPoint by advocating the military strategy of training cavalry units in effective sabre fighting, a skill perfected by the Russian Cossack Dragoons. The Colonel was brutally explicit in his views on how warfare against the Indians should be conducted and among many of his uncompromising statements was that the warlike tribes should be annihilated by military force employing a policy of 'No Prisoners.' On presidential orders Stone was promoted General with immediate effect and with a cavalry force of over five hundred and fifty elite troops and supporting auxiliaries he moved westwards and was to be afforded, by Presidential Order, all possible support from commanders of forts already in the locale of his mission. Viewed with apprehension and suspicion by veteran Indian fighters already in the field, General B. Stone was no fool and the way in which he deployed his force showed the mettle of the man. By using the available Indian

Scouts already in the service of the military, Gen. Stone was able to forge a temporary agreement with the Commanche War Council, instigated originally by Ten Bears of great warrior renown, to allow his force to pursue and engage the Apaches under Yellow Snake without interference.

General Stone then bivouaced his troops in an unusual formation of an outer ring with blocks of troops within the circle. He stationed this encampment slap bang in the middle of the open terrain of desert scrubland frequented by the Apaches thus in effect issuing a direct challenge to Yellow Snake. Full strength patrols comprising fifty cavalry troopers under an officer and a sergeant made regular sweeps of the area to combat and engage Indian raiding parties. Other units of similar size were held in alert readiness to be deployed as necessary. He waited for a reaction and he did not have to wait long. It started with just a minor skirmish near the outward bound trail for Silver City where a patrol encountered a band of several dozen Apaches lying in ambush for a wagon train of settlers riding their 'Prairie Schooners' westwards. The Indians were surprised by the cavalry's new tactics of using the terrain for concealment as they emerged fast from a ravine and came upon them suddenly. A pitched battle developed in which the Apaches were unable to reach their ponies concealed nearby. Caught on foot the warriors were no match for the slashing sabres and were cut to pieces. Only a bare few wounded braves made it back to inform Yellow Snake.

Gen. Stone was delighted by this outcome and now proceeded to implement the next phase of his strategy. Second guessing that Yellow Snake would react by attacking his encampment he divided his force into three camps each with an outer ring and blocks of ten within the circle. The circles were set in a triangular disposition with a space between them in the middle which Stone referred to, with a brutal laugh, as the 'Death Zone.' All the cavalry units were put on high alert as the cryptic command 'Sharpen Sabres' echoed throughout the ranks.

With the last rays of a blood red sun bathing the desert scrubland, Yellow Snake attacked in full force committing around two hundred fighting braves on foot to penetrate the cavalry positions. Taken aback at first by the change in the enemy soldier's camp positions Yellow Snake nonetheless pushed forward the raid with a vengeance gloating at the prospect of gaining further arms and ammunition not to mention horses for his ultimate conquest of the hated whites. At first the Apaches achieved significant breakthroughs and vicious Indian warriors who showed no fear inflicted heavy casualties as in disciplined bands they raided the perimeters of each encampment at the same time. Inevitably as Stone had predicted they began to mass in the centre of his three camp disposition and that is when he sprung his trap. At a pre-arranged bugle blast signal from Stone's command quarters echoed by similar bugle calls within the remaining circles, double line formations of cavalry now joined up the three camps forming one large impenetrable circle which enclosed the Apache forces. There was no way out and no surrender accepted. The slaughter was horrendous as the sabre slashing horsemen, armed also with handguns, revelled in the bloody revenge they inflicted on the Apaches. When the warriors realised they were trapped they began to run wildly amok and succeeded in some killing and injuring of troopers and horses before being cut down themselves. A few with reservation living backgrounds made to surrender, hoping to live to rape and fight another day but the cavalry soldiers were well aware of the General's instructions 'No Prisoners' and in any case were reminiscent of fellow blue coats killed and burned at Fort Commanche. The men were in no mood to be merciful and so these ex-reservation Apaches were butchered along with the rest. In some areas of the battlefield the fighting was so intense that no quarter was given by either side and the ground ran red with blood which reflected starkly in the firelight from some of the burning tents. In the midst of the fighting Yellow Snake succumbed to the inevitable and striking out at a passing cavalryman he took the soldier's horse and with a defiant war cry succeeded in escaping the melee of combatants; some few others likewise achieved a lucky exit from the kill zone. But the majority of the Apaches were doomed and died where they stood and fought. There were many trooper casualties but this was an insignificant number in comparison to the Indian dead. Slasher Stone had won his war and although the Commanche now still had free rein around the Rio Grande area to raid and rampage, the Apache presence was totally neutralised. Stone would be hailed the hero back in Washington circles and no doubt would be duly honoured.

SLAYCO MOUNTS A WARPARTY

Ben viewed these events with considerable concern and interest and when he learned on the Indian grapevine that Yellow Snake had escaped with his life and was now alone and a fugitive, he knew that his time to act had come. With this in mind he requested to see the Commanding Officer, Colonel J.B. Jefferson, a gruff veteran of the Indian Campaigns. Ben put forward a proposal in which he volunteered to take a small detachment of selected troopers and an Indian Tracker, no more than five in all, and pursue Yellow Snake with a view to capturing or killing him. The Colonel stood up from his desk and confronted Ben soberly.

"Lieutenant, you're young and inexperienced. I appreciate your spirit but this Indian, Yellow Snake, is a ruthless desperado of the worst possible kind and it will take a highly organised military campaign, similar to the one General Stone just recently concluded, to flush him out. At present we do not have the resources to mount such a campaign and I doubt whether it would succeed if we had. Now I know something of your history, Ben, and I realise this is something of a personal issue for you, what with the death of your father and all, but if I sent you off with small detail I'd be sending you to your death. Forget it, my boy. You'll make a fine officer, Ben, one who has much more important things to do than chase some crazy Indian. Leave that sort of thing to cold blooded killers like Bruce Stone and his Slashers."

Ben looked at this kindly man whom he knew only meant well but after long consideration he knew that this was something he had to do or die trying. As calmly as he could he told the Colonel of his determination and that he was so adamant that, if necessary, he was prepared to resign his commission. Colonel Jefferson sighed and resumed his seat. He sat a while with his head in his hands deep in thought. Aware of Ben's Washington connections he felt obliged to offer the young man something positive. Then abruptly he leaned back in his chair and stared at Ben who was still dutifully standing before him.

"I'm going out on a limb over this but I am authorising you to take indefinite unpaid leave of absence to carry out whatever it is you have in mind. Pray let it be successful and you return to normal duties and your career. No one, I repeat no one must know of this arrangement which is to be our secret. I will, of course, write up an official note to this effect which will be entered in the Fort Log for the

Officer Commanding's eyes only in case anything happens to me. My advice to you, young fellow, is to forget the whole thing but if otherwise then see you take some expert advice. I believe you know Abe Jenson who is here recuperating from wounds he received in Phoenix. He has a wealth of experience of Indian fighting and tracking hostiles. Confide in him and listen to his opinion of how you might go about this thing which he is sure to agree with me is foolhardy in the extreme. Now that is all except to wish you God speed. You are dismissed."

Having said his piece the Colonel turned his chair and stared out at the empty parade ground. Ben, overwhelmed by this man's generosity, could only say a heartfelt thankyou and with a respectful salute left the room. Once outside he felt exhilarated. The mission he had so long fostered in his mind was about to become reality and now he had the go-head he began to feel that sinking feeling of wondering just how he might carry it all through. The Colonel was correct. He needed advice and Jenson was the right man to see. When he inquired the big man's whereabouts he was directed to the fort medical centre. A log cabin served as the hospital area and it was in one of the side rooms that Ben found his erstwhile rescuer and friend.

After a few pleasantries and commiserating with him over his wounds which were only slight, Ben briefly outlined his plans to the old Texas Ranger and awaited his reaction. Jenson stared long and hard at Ben before saying:

"So you're going after Yellow Snake?" It was more a statement than a question.

"Well Sonny you'd better be ten times the man I think you are, and then some, if you expect to tangle with the most ornery, murderous, rapist son of a bitch that ever came out of an Apache Squaw."

"It's something I've got to do, that's all" Ben said quietly.

The big man squirmed in his seat and winced at the pain in his side.

"Well then, seems like you've got yourself one hell of a problem, Ben."

"I thought you might offer me some advice."

"Sure, don't do it! Forget the whole thing. Go back to your folks in Washington and pick yourself out one of them society beauties and get hitched. Makes more sense than chasing after an hombre like Yellow Snake and getting yourself kilt more than likely."

"Abe, I've made up my mind and I've set my sights on going through with this whether I get help or not. Thanks for seeing me. You never know I might just pull it off. Anyway, so long for now." And with a farewell grin Ben moved towards the door.

"Now hold your horses I didn't say I wouldn't help. I just needed to find out how set you are on this fool's caper and if you couldn't be persuaded to drop the whole thing to figure out what to tell you so you'd best settle yourself down, listen and listen real good."

"Did the Colonel have a word with you?"

"You bet your life he did cos he reckons you're plumb crazy and I agree with him."

Ben eased himself back into a chair and looked at Jenson as the Big Man frowned and leaned forward in his seat with a deadly serious expression on his face.

"First you got to decide what you're aiming to do. In my book that means a killing. Nobody's gonna rope and tie this Indian. When you catch up with him, kill him quick or he'll kill you. You got that straight?" Ben nodded

Next, once you find his trail, mind what signals you give off. If you need a fire dig a hole and use only dry wood, no green, that makes smoke. Make it around noon when everywhere's so hot the heat from your fire will be lost in the haze. Never light a fire at night it will only tell your enemy where you are. Dig a hole when you squat and bury it. Oh, Yellow Snake's gonna find out you're tailing him. Indians have a way of knowing like it's a message on the wind." Here Jenson made a circling motion with his hand above his head.

"Sure he'll soon tell you're after him only don't deal him no aces. He'll set traps for you so beware. Keep to the high ground, ride just below a ridge, stay away from canyons and ravines where he can double back and ambush you. Don't shoot off your guns at anything less you have to. Sounds of gunfire travel far in desert and mountain country."

Jenson paused, taking time to light a cigar, letting his words sink in. Ben took the opportunity to ask a question.

"What guns should I take?"

"Carry a Colt .45, some spare shells in a holster belt. You still got that Bowie Knife your Pa left you?"

Ben nodded.

"Good, use it for digging but keep it sheathed in the sun less it reflects your position. Get yourself a repeating rifle, mebbe a Winchester like the '73. Pick yourself a pair of unshod ponies from the herd the Cavalry rounded up after Slasher Stone's victory. An unshod horse makes little sound even on rocks. Use one for a pack horse. Load plenty hard tack, beans and coffee. Two canteens, grain for the horses and a blanket or two for sleepin. It gets mighty cold out there at night."

It seemed that all had been said that needed saying. Ben had noted every word and he felt exhilarated at the possibility of putting it all into practice. It had freed his mind from the problem of thinking he couldn't make it work. Then as he was about to take his leave Jenson stood and, although he was favouring the wound in his side, Ben was impressed once more by the size and power emanating from this man who had not only proved his saviour once but was now rendering this new endeavour with the knowledge that would give it a chance to work. He was about to say how grateful he was when Jenson cut him short.

"Jest cos Ah told you HOW don't mean you can carry it off when it comes to the DOING. You got to think more like an Indian than a white man. If it comes to a shootin, take your time, don't try for a head shot til he's down. I once heard John Wesley Hardin sounding off in some bar room but something of what he said stuck in my mind as making real good horse sense: 'Speed of draw is fine but accuracy of shot is final.' I reckon he should know having killed around thirty men. If this Apache hits you first then last him out in which case it pays to have an edge." Jenson stretched out his right hand and thrust it inside the open top cowhide vest he was wearing and brought out a short double barrelled Derringer pistol attached to a cord around his neck. It was the kind of gun favoured by card players because it could fit comfortable inside a waistcoat pocket and yet was lethal when fired at close range.

"Hang this around your neck, use it as a last resort. And another thing, you remember Dan Blue Feather? Just so you'll know him when he you meet up, he is half Indian, wears a flat black hat and has two pig tails, one each side of his face. Well it seems he heard what you did for Wichita; they were good friends. I'm gonna ask him to set you right on Yellow Snake's trail then leave you to finish it now I've kinda got wind of what you are about to attempt and I know that Dan will help. Listen to him real good and he'll set you right. Now Mister that is all 'cepting to advise you to make ready soon, no sense in hanging around so word gets out 'bout what you're aiming to do. Leave before dawn. Dan is sure to catch up with you in his own time. Good luck. In two months if I haven't heard from you I'll come lookin fer what's left."

Ben thanked his big friend and hurried away. He had much to prepare and he couldn't wait to get started lest his courage ran out as, after the talk with Abe Jenson, revealed to him, the enormity of the task he faced. But an iron will drove Ben Slayco and he would not forego the task he had set himself

HITTING THE TRAIL

Three nights after his session with Jenson, Ben rode out of Fort Sumner mounted on a sturdy war pony captured from the defeated Indian hoard led by Yellow Snake. A lead tether attached another pony packed with provisions for the hunt. The horses might have seemed small, standing at barely twelve hands high in comparison to the cavalry mounts which were larger, but these ponies came from mustang stock, a breed forged by nature to withstand the extremes of the desert wilderness and survive the worst weather conditions imaginable. He was as well equipped as he could manage in view of the time available and his limited financial resources. It was an hour and a half after midnight when he took the desert trail under a sliver of silver moon which, if he was looking for a portent, looked mighty like a sabre shining out against a dark sky. No one witnessed his departure except a gruff trooper guarding the gates.

The terrain all around him looked grey and deceptively flat concealing ravines and dried stream beds which could hide an enemy force as easily as a pack of wolves. Suddenly, as if rising from nowhere, Dan Blue Feather, true to Jenson's promise, joined him on the trail. The men exchanged greeting gestures but no words were spoken as was common between travellers. The sound of words, like the light for a cigar, could travel far and give you away. His mission was only just beginning but it was already on a war footing. As they headed further out they came across the rotting bodies of dead horses. Sorely wounded in battle they had bolted into the desert and desperately galloped away until their bodies broke and they dropped to die a lingering death. Here and there the riders spotted the tawny shape of Mexican wolves scavenging the carcasses. Several miles on Blue Feather dismounted to examine closely the sign he had spotted. Bent double and leading his horse he tracked the trail for some distance before mounting up again and heading east. Ben dutifully followed, his faith in this man's skills assured. They pushed on 'til noon the following day before stopping to give the horses a break and feed them some grain. They had left the desert behind and were now on the prairie. A sea of grasses wavered before them in the wind. This was lush cattle country where herds of buffalo sometimes roamed. The men drank black unsweetened coffee from a tin jug heated over a fire made from dry buffalo dung and ate hardtack. Blue Feather, never one to waste words, pointed to a distant blur on the horizon and said briefly.

"Him run straight like lone wolf for cover. Old places now bad medicine. Look for new place, new mountain, make new power."

"How far is he ahead of us Dan?"

"Mebbe two, three days. He following cattle drive trails east to cover his tracks."

"Where do you think he's headed?"

"Go where no Apaches go. Safe from Commanche, safe from Blue Coats."

"But where can he go?"

Blue Feather did not at first answer. Then he cast around with his eyes as if the earth and the sky would inform him. Finally he picked up a handful of the sandy ground and sifted it through his hands with a faraway look in his eyes before turning to Ben.

"Old ones in tribe sing songs of old times when Apache lived far from home in place where many streams come from white river. People called Caddo, Osage, many names. High Ridge Mountains, sweet water country, Whites call place Ozarks. This place where mebbe Yellow Snake now go."

"That's one hell of a journey, clear to Missouri Country. Why it's North of Wichita by way of Tulsa even."

"Still Indian Country."

Blue Feather said spreading both arms wide. Yellow Snake mebbe remember women singings of Land of White Water.

Ben mulled over what Dan had said. It made sense because Yellow Snake would realise that he'd be hunted and if he returned to his usual haunts he'd likely be captured or killed now that his war bands were scattered and defeated.

"Dan I reckon you're right so let's ride him down."

Blue Feather rarely smiled but now he allowed himself a slight grin at the young man's gung ho enthusiasm as both men rode North by East following the trail of their elusive quarry.

TAKING FLIGHT

Far along the cattle trails Yellow Snake took time to pause and reflect on what had happened to him. The feelings were bitter sour in his mouth causing him to spit out his hatred of the detestable white men who were stealing the land which belonged to his people. He had made his escape from the seething battle ground only as a last resort once he saw that defeat was inevitable. He would live to fight another day and he would have revenge. But for now he must ensure his own survival. The cavalry horse he had taken was a strong hardy mount that would carry him far especially since he had stripped it of the heavy saddle and large campaign saddle bags that to his mind were unnecessary. He rode Indian style with only a rough blanket beneath him. He was heading along the white eye's cattle trail partly to cover his tracks from pursuit by any but the most skilful hunters but also to find his way to the ancestral mountain refuge that the old people sang about in the wickiups of his childhood. His enemies would expect him to have fled south to the Apache hideouts in Mexico. Safe in the mountains ahead he would wait his time and then summon those who had survived the blue coat's massacre to join him again to follow the war trail.

HARD ON THE TRAIL

After three day's rough riding Ben and Dan Blue Feather struck a rest camp by a gushing stream in the foothills which lay at the foot of the Ozark rocky ridges and mountains. They bathed in the white water pools, feasted on fresh game and put their horses to grazing. After a full day of relaxing Blue Feather left the camp at dawn the next morning to search for signs of Yellow Snake. He returned triumphant in late afternoon to announce that he'd found the Indian's tracks about two miles from their base and that they were not more than a day old. Over a meal of ring tailed deer meat and fresh cooked dough biscuits with coffee, they discussed a strategy for Ben to follow which served to reinforce what Jenson had already advised. Then the half breed looked across the fire at Ben, his dark sombre eyes reflecting the firelight and Ben guessed what he was about to say.

"This war not my war. Your war. Better you hunt alone. Catch him. Kill him quick. Take his power."

Ben nodded agreement. He thanked the half breed for his help in tracking Yellow Snake and the breed said he owed it because of what Ben did for his friend, the Wichita Kid. In the cool of the morning Ben awoke to find he was alone. Dan Blue Feather had left sometime earlier without a sound in the mysterious way of his mother's race. As he threw back his blanket he discover a piece of rawhide on which a knife had marked out a rough sketch of where Ben could find the start of Yellow Snake's trail.

"I reckon anyway he's gonna be headed uphill to that mountain range; that's where we'll meet up." Ben said to himself. On the stretch of the horizon above him Ben could just make out a blurred blue line that denoted the mountain fastness which he could feel was now all wrapped up in his looming destiny.

Ben took his time saddling and packing the horses. They were restive and eager to be off. He'd already checked his Colt Revolver and had fully loaded the Winchester Rifle. In one of his shirt pockets he put four .32 bullets for the loaded Derringer he wore Jenson style on a cord around his neck. If he had to fire it he doubted whether there would be time to reload but he carried the bullets just in case. To his mind he was ready for action come what may.

To start with the going was easy. Deer tracks bordered the numerous streams that fed the big White River that tumbled and splashed over a rocky bed. Myriad flocks of birds he had never seen before flashed their coloured wings as they flew across his path. Soon he arrived at the point on Danny's sketch map that marked the beginning of the trail left by Yellow Snake. Even Ben's sharp eyes were able to pick out faint hoof prints left by a shod cavalry horse. The tracks meandered alongside a stony stream that wound away upwards into the near distance. The sun shining down from the mountain tops was now full in his face so he skirted a nearby ridge to take advantage of the shadows cast by a line of tall standing trees. Other than wildlife there were no signs of mankind. As the route became steeper the trail was strewn with stony debris which made riding harder and as the path dipped and rose through pockets of shadow and sunlight he dismounted and led the horses on foot over the rocky terrain. Moving up into the depth of the Ozarks country Ben Slayco felt strangely alone as he plied his mission. The only sounds he heard among the craggy ridges were the sounds of his horses attempting to find a footing in the shale, the creak of the saddle and the leathery slap of the saddle bags against the flanks of his horse. As the day wore on the sun swung round and burned hot at his back. He made camp for the night early making sure he couldn't be seen from above. It was a cold camp since he couldn't risk a fire. He hobbled the horses close to a patch of fresh grass next to a stand of trees through which a shallow rushing stream raced downhill. It was a land of plentiful water and thick vegetation was abundant on the craggy hillsides and this afforded him and the horses excellent cover. It would also, he noted, be to the advantage of his quarry of which Ben had seen no further sign following the discovery of the hoof prints. But it was early days into his quest, Ben reflected, time enough soon for the denouement. Night enfolded the camp and Ben lay on his back enraptured by the sight of millions of stars brightening the dark sky in advance of the rising of the moon so different from the skies filled with camp fire smoke which polluted the air above Fort Sumner. As the full moon rose and silvered the landscape he turned on his side to sleep. Near to his his right hand lay the loaded Colt .45, on his belt the broad Bowie Knife nestled comfortably in the small of his back. He would never sleep totally at ease until his purpose was completed.

THE KILLING GROUNDS

About two miles North of where Ben slept Yellow Snake had a problem. His prized bow had been lost in the battle in the desert. Now that he had successfully made his escape he felt it was the time to replace it. On the way up to his present position he had noticed some young saplings growing alongside a stream bed. Once dried in the sun and worked on with his knife one of them would make a fine bow to silently hunt game. Tonight there was to be a full moon, the kind Apaches called a stalking moon since it was easy to read tracks by its light. Roping his horse to a tree he set out to run back to where he'd seen the saplings. He was now well into his prime years but he still prided himself on the fitness of his body. Apache braves could run many miles without stopping to rest, some boasted they could run fifty miles in a day and even outrun a horse and, of course, warriors always fought on foot. Yellow Snake smoothly covered the distance to the stream where the saplings grew but when he arrived there he suffered a shock. There in the soft mud of the game trails in the bright light of the moon he saw the traces of two unshod ponies alongside the remnants of his own horse tracks. The sight sent his mind into a whirl. He was being tracked and tailed, there was no doubt about it. Even here he might not be safe. With a watchful eye on the trail he hastily cut several of the young saplings. As his mind calmed after the revelation that he was being hunted he changed to a more aggressive mode. It was fortunate that he had by chance found these tracks for now he could turn the discovery to his advantage. He would seek out and kill this new enemy but he decided against inviting a confrontation

Wild Adventures in Time and Place

at this moment in time. His weapons apart from his knife were back where he'd hidden his horse. Better to wait, he thought, alerted to the danger now he would set an ambush tomorrow and take this hunter out. Swiftly and soundlessly he ran back to his camp.

⁂

Ben Slayco rose early as the dawn light lit up the crags around him. He filled his canteen from the stream and drank thirstily of the sweet mountain water. Breakfast consisted of hard tack and jerky, dried beef. As he saddled his horse he thought that today might just prove to be the one to find and kill Yellow Snake. With this in mind he double checked his weapons. He intended to ride the high country today and look for sign. As he negotiated one after another of the game trails that led him higher into the Ozarks he experienced a shift in the air temperature from morning cool to noontime hot. At one point he halted below a range of hills that overlooked a deep river valley overgrown with trees and bushes. Squinting against the harsh sunlight his gaze roved across the expanse beneath the looming mountain chain when all of a sudden his eyes caught a reflected flash of silver. Instantly reacting and true to his military training he dove down and rolled across the hard ground just as his horse squealed at the impact of a heavy calibre bullet. Two further shots punctured the side of the incline against which he'd been silhouetted. Regaining his senses after the shock of the rifle fire Ben scrambled towards the shelter of the body of his dead horse. Grabbing the Winchester from the scabbard attached to his saddle he squirmed to a firing position and stared down the valley. He quickly spotted a rider galloping full pelt up the valley side towards him. It was Yellow Snake mounted on a cavalry steed and he was coming at speed to finish him off. Winded and still suffering the shock of the unexpected attack, Ben loosed off two rapid fire shots at the approaching horseman. His aim was impromptu and shaky but it served to arrest the advancing Indian although the bullets went wide of their target. A furtive glance confirmed that his adversary had disappeared. But for Ben it was now a moment of intense realisation. Somehow Yellow Snake had got wind that he was being pursued and had taken retaliatory action. He'd set an ambush and it would have done for him but for a freak reflection off the butt of the Apache's rifle. The bullet that killed his pony and the others that hit the rocks were meant for him and from now on he would need to be doubly cautious. Only a momentary glint from the rifle had saved him. It had to have been his father's rifle, the one with the silver presentation plate set in the wood of the butt. Strange to think that except for that silver plate he could have been killed. Ben waited a full hour before moving. Then satisfied that no further attacks were impending he quickly stripped his saddle and other livery from the dead horse and concealed them as best he could amid some boulders. The saddle bags containing some dried food and spare ammunition he loaded onto his pack horse which had become spooked by the shots and run off some distance. Then leading the pony by hand and wary of ambush he searched for a safe place to hide and gather his wits. Tonight would be full of danger since Yellow Snake would be tracking him as soon as the moon rose. So Ben felt he had two options: either stay and fight or make a run for it now that his mission had been discovered. Well perhaps he could think out a way to turn his predicament to an advantage. For the present he continued searching for a suitable hide, perhaps a cave or deep crevice in the rocks where he could hole-up and devise a plan. Then he had a sudden brainwave. In the distance he spotted a small narrow plateau which afforded a view over the whole area and, more important for the plan he was considering, could be seen from anywhere and everywhere around.

On arriving at the selected place he proceeded to unpack the pony, fed him some grain, gave him water from one of the canteens and hobbled him to prevent straying. Then gathering as much dry wood as he could he lit a huge fire and, as dusk was beginning to set in, he built the fire into a fierce blaze which he reckoned could be seen for miles. With deliberate forethought he set out cooking utensils and arranged his baggage to resemble a sleeping figure. Then before it became fully dark he quickly cooked himself some bacon and coffee to ward off the cold night he intended to spend awake and waiting. After his meal he banked his campfire with further tree falls, tested the wind direction and furtively prepared to leave. Satisfied that he had arranged everything just right, he took his rifle and a blanket and concealed himself in a cluster of boulders about a hundred yards from his fire, upwind so that his scent would not carry. Now he waited. The trap was set. For his ambush to work Yellow Snake would have to see his fire and reckon that he was dealing with a dude, possibly an itinerant bounty hunter who had recklessly exposed himself on the morning. Now this man had built a fire that defied common sense and identified his position for all to see. But if the Apache smelt a trap then he was doomed.

As the hours ticked by waiting became an agony of tortured muscles unused to staying rigid in the same position for so long. At one point he dozed off only to be jerked awake with frightening suddenness. Not sure what had caused him to awaken Ben stared around wildly. The blackness saturated the scene since the moon was not yet up. Then as he stared hard into the night he caught sight of a dim shape which sent his heart pounding. The outline of a figure became faintly visible in the all enclosing darkness. Red bronzed skin reflected just enough light from the glowing embers of the fire to be identifiable. An image emerged to Ben's straining vision of a breech clout clad form standing tall and wearing the yellow headband above the menacing eyes of the most dangerous Indian Ben would ever face. It was Yellow Snake in person come to call and render death. Cool headed now that the moment of truth had arrived at long last to revenge the death of his father at the hands of this savage, Ben eased his Winchester stealthily forward and, taking careful aim, he squeezed the trigger. A fateful premonition caused Yellow Snake to leap to one side as the shot rang out but not quickly enough to escape a bullet wound to the left shoulder. Instantly he vanished into the night. Ben immediately jumped up jerking his cramped limbs into action when Jenson's words of warning stopped him in his tracks.

"If you hit him and he doesn't go down, don't go galloping after him cos he'll be waiting to slit your guts. A wounded Apache is worse than a wounded cougar. Let him bleed some. Wait a couple of hours then go after him."

Jenson's caution sobered Ben's elation and slowed his impetuosity. He moved to the fire and poured himself a welcome coffee. He needed two hands to control his cup as a bout of shaking excited his body. He would wait till dawn then finish the job as best he could. He was thrilled that his trap had worked. It proved that Yellow Snake was not invulnerable and the realisation gave him confidence that he could pull the whole thing off despite some earlier misgivings.

Ben stayed awake all night in case the Apache mounted an immediate counter attack. At morning's first light he set out to track him down. There was blood spoor everywhere in the immediate vicinity of the camp. Yellow Snake had been hit bad and Ben was able to follow the path of his escape with ease for about a mile as the wounded Indian negotiated a rocky trail which eventually terminated at a gushing waterfall. On closer scrutiny it seemed as if after washing it he had plastered his wound with mud from the clay deposits at the side of the stream. But then the tracks disappeared amongst the rocks and scrub bushes growing there. Ben surmised that Yellow Snake had probably climbed over the top of the water fall after dressing his wound but even though he worked the ground in ever widening circles he could find no trace of him. The Apache had obviously gone to earth somewhere and was probably holed up in a cave. Frustrated and exhausted through the efforts of the night and the lack of sleep Ben could not help letting it all out in a rip roaring rebel yell that he hoped would carry to the ears of the Apache and spook him so that he would know that his end was near. Feeling relieved he decided to return to his camp and rest up a while to recover his strength and decide what to do next.

Approaching the camp along the high ridge he had selected to trap Yellow Snake he should have noticed earlier that all was not right but his senses were fogged by fatigue and hunger and he was not alerted to the danger until it was almost too late. The sight that greeted him struck a note of horror which throbbed through his body with sickening dread. His one remaining pony lay on its side amidst a pool of blood seeping from its ripped throat and over its dead body stood the terrifying figure of Yellow Snake armed with a long pole he had fashioned from a sapling. He had doubled back as Ben was searching for him. His stance was a challenge to the younger man. He wanted to kill Ben with his bare hands to redress the ignominy of failing to detect the trap that had almost killed him. At the sight Ben dropped his rifle and lunged to draw his six gun but Yellow Snake was quicker and struck him a disabling blow with the stave knocking him to the ground and sending the Colt flying out of reach. Ben scrambled to his feet and closed with the Apache grabbing the pole before it could hit him again. Nauseated by the pungent animal smell of the Apache's body Ben jammed his elbow into the clay covering the bullet wound on Yellow Snake's chest. At the blow the Indian screeched a scream through his clenched teeth and furiously grabbed Ben around the shoulders and hurled him to the ground. Quick as a flash Ben was on his feet again and the two men closed in wrestling combat. Ben was young and powerfully built but he was no match for his adversary. Apache children learn to wrestle with each other from the earliest age and Ben found himself overwhelmed by Yellow Snake's superior skills. The end of the fight came fast and furious as Ben was lifted high in the air above the Apache's head and dashed with body wrenching force to the ground. Then Yellow Snake backed off and drew a wicked looking curved knife from his waist band and with an evil leer moved towards his opponent. Ben, badly winded and hurting all over, scrambled to a sitting position with his back against a boulder and desperately fumbled and groped in his shirt for Jenson's Derringer. Just as the Apache stooped to gut him from crotch to throat Ben at last retrieved the weapon and, stretching out his arm, cocked the hammers and squeezed both triggers, firing point blank up into Yellow Snake's face. The Apache was knocked upright by the force of the gun blast and the impact of the bullets. The Indian stood erect for a long moment with only the trace of incomprehension on his face, then he slowly crumbled and dropped dead before his body hit the ground. One of the Derringer .32 heavy slugs had penetrated his left eye the other had bored a neat hole in his forehead before leaving with a massive exit wound at the rear.

For a long time Ben didn't move, couldn't move. He just sat there with the dead body of the Indian at his feet. It was all over but it had been touch and go. But for the Big Man's Derringer he would be dead. Ben heaved a massive sigh and slumped totally spent both physically and mentally. His body could take no more and he slipped into a deep sleep where he sat. It was some hours before he awoke. Rousing himself erect he stood over Yellow Snakes lifeless form and prised the evil looking knife from the Apache's hand, then he bent down and cut away the yellow headband from the Indian's forehead. This with the Indian's knife would be the only memento he would keep. The body he would leave as carcass meat for the wolves and buzzards. Now he needed to find Yellow Snake's horse and there was also something special he wanted from the Apache's camp.

It took Ben over two hours of tracking back and forth until he found Yellow Snake's camp and then it was only through the whinnying alarm cries of the cavalry horse which enabled him to discover the well camouflaged hideout. By a crevice in a rock lay a rifle, a Spencer Presentation model of 1866. He recognised at once the firearm his father had carried with pride and which had been taken from him at his death. On the silver mounted plaque his father's name was inscribed. Tears welled in his eyes for his lost father as he read

"Presented to Lt. Col. Joshua B. Howard in recognition of Outstanding Leadership and Valour."

Here at last he could claim his father's name that had been owed to him all along. From this moment on he'd be known as Ben Howard and the mystical tag 'Slayco' could forever be dropped as just part of a bad dream that ended with the death of Yellow Snake. His life's quest had peaked and there was nothing else left to be resolved

Ben packed only the minimum provisions from the dead pony in the saddle bags retrieved with the saddle from where he'd cached them in the rocks. The horse seemed glad to see him and he fed it grain and watered it before heading down the hills past the white water streams. When he reached the foot of the hills he turned his horse due west out across the prairie towards Fort Sumner. Before he'd covered two miles he was joined by Dan Blue Feather. On meeting him the half breed simply struck his chest with a downward clenched fist sign that meant 'It is finished.' Ben nodded without speaking and the two men took their time on the journey back. A mile out from the Fort Dan Blue Feather waved 'Adios' and rode away. As Ben entered the compound and dismounted he was surprised to be greeted with a hearty back slap by Jenson.

"So you did it! We're right proud of you Ben. You took on one hell of a mission."

"How did you know?"

"We've known for some days now, don't ask me how but our resident Indians started an impromptu death song act about three days ago. They said it was for a great war chief, an Apache brother who had been killed that day."

"But how could they know" Ben asked.

"It sure beats me pal but there's been a heap of Apache smoke signals on the horizon. All I know is they got ways of finding out about things. Mebbe it's written on the wind or in the sky or something. C'm on and let me buy you a drink and you can tell me all about it."

And so it was that Jenson got the whole story and also got his Derringer back. He held it reverently for a short while and then drily remarked:

"Wadda you know. The gun that shot Yellow Snake. Oughta be worth hanging onto." Then in a serious voice he finally said:

"Ben, you sure were one hell of a lucky son-of-a-bitch."

Ben nodded and reiterated his thanks for the loan of the small gun which had saved his life.

"You're mighty welcome" Abe Jenson said with an approving smile.

⁓

And so the saga of Slayco's Warparty ended and Lt. Ben Shennigan Howard travelled back east to take up a new post far away from the wild western frontier where he'd earned his laurels. Only whenever and wherever he looked at a red and orange sunset his mind was momentarily swept back there to his memories and he fancied he could smell the mesquite and hear the roar of the desert wind and then feel he was again on the back of an Indian war pony riding the prairie that seemed to stretch on forever. He would make no more war parties.

⁓

The Wolf Research Agenda

She dashed out from the shadows between the towering dark buildings, bolting with wild desperation and terror. Behind the smoking ruin of her car straddled the narrow street. She had escaped barely seconds before it was blasted apart by devastating gunfire. She had already cast her high heels to run faster in her stocking feet. She was young and fit and raced in headlong flight towards the streetlights ahead, her long hair streaming out behind as she clutched a briefcase against her body. Two tall dark figures slowly gained on her in relentless pursuit. Finally, as she sprinted across the dingy opening of a narrow ally way she was caught in a murderous cross fire which caused her body to blaze in a blinding flash. She hadn't even had time to scream. What remained of her lay smouldering in the gutter. One of the killers approached and without a glance at the smouldering heap, stooped and retrieved the briefcase from the roadway where it had been hurled by the impact of the shots. Then the two of them silently faded away into the night. From the shadowed recesses of a corner, beneath a pile of cardboard and newspaper, a shocked white face had witnessed the end of the chase and the killing.

In the high security basement of a building in the heart of London, the Chief of the Intelligence Services for the League, a covert agency, was scanning a FOR YOUR EYES ONLY report just faxed directly to his desk. He grunted with satisfaction as he read the bottom line:

TARGET ELIMINATED. DISC RETRIEVED

D.C.I. Jack Harwood accompanied by D.S. Lynn Forest, having thoroughly checked the murder scene and sent for a forensics team, were now back at base jointly interviewing the tramp known as "Wino" who had identified himself as a witness to the uniformed officers first at the scen e. At the conclusion of the short statement taken down by Sergeant Forest, the witness, who refused to give a name other than 'Wino,' made an alarming observation. "It wasn't human, Guv". Startled, Harwood `asked "Do you mean that what happened was inhuman?" "No!" came the reply "I meant that them that did it weren't human. I got a good look at the one who picked up the girl's case, he had the face of a monster, like something from outer space". "You'd been drinking all day?" Harwood queried. "I know what I seen. It scared me sober. I know what I seen" were the angry retorts. The two officers stared blankly at each other in consternation. "Well that narrows the field of suspects"

Harwood said. "There can't be that many space monsters wandering around London." "You hope" said the Tramp ominously as he rose to leave.

༄

Agent Wilcox, whose roles included office manager, secretary and personal bodyguard to the Chief- Code Name Scorpio- entered the private inner sanctum without knocking as was her privilege, and confronted him with the latest news. "They've got him!" Scorpio glared at her. She stared back stonily, unfazed by his manner which at the best of times was overbearing. He saw before him the tall solid frame of a mature woman, conservatively dressed, who evidenced seniority by her bearing and the fierceness in her eyes. "Let's go," he barked and, moving like a big cat, she followed him stopping only to collect the loaded 9mm Glock semi-automatic pistol from a desk drawer.

The windowless basement cell-like room they entered stank of sweat and other body smells but neither of them flinched. Two huge humanoid figures were stripped to the waist, their grey muscular bodies and huge eyes glistened in the dazzling lights, their hands shone red with blood and gore from the tortured victim who sat strapped naked to an iron chair bolted to the floor. "Well" the chief hissed. One of the torturers answered in a hollow metallic sounding voice: "He will not tell!" The Chief responded with unadulterated venom. "Keep him alive until you find out or it will be the worse, and I mean the very worst for both of you" he growled with a malicious snarl. As he and Wilcox left the room, unearthly screams followed them, abruptly ceasing as the soundproofed door whirred shut behind them.

The following morning the two Detectives collected the report on their case from Forensics:-

F.A.O.
D.C.I. Harwood.

Forensic Findings Summary: Examination of victim revealed no D.N.A. due to burned state of body parts. Murder scene inspection yielded fire-damaged silver bracelet bearing the engraved name, Martha Kaley. Further enquiries identified her as a freelance journalist, specialising in science topics mainly for the broadsheets. No trace of assailants found…………….. End.

After reading the report, Harwood and Forest looked at each other and shrugged "Someone, somewhere knows what she was doing and isn't telling." "And" Forest said "someone else knew and got to her". "Perhaps" mused Harwood. "Or she could have been investigating something on her own and rattled someone's cage. Someone with clout." Forest paled and gave a little shiver. \

"There's another package here for you. Looks important, person to person she said. Came this afternoon just as I arrived; had to show my badge and sign for it." "Well let's see what's in it" said Harwood. "It's already been checked for devices" continued Forest. Harwood nodded and added dryly "Thanks for telling me" as he opened the parcel to find a DVD carefully wrapped, unlabelled and without any notice of the sender.

Intrigued, they immediately pulled on latex examination gloves so as not to destroy any evidence. "I have a hunch that this could be related to our current investigations," he said pointedly. Just then a male colleague entered the room and hailed them: "Hey you two, look sharp, the Super Super Dooper wants to see you, pronto!"

In response to the flashing alert light, Scorpio reached across his maple wood desk and clicked open the communications console. The metallic voice informed him that the object they were seeking had been sent by special delivery to a Scotland Yard Detective, Chief Inspector Harwood. "Good work" was the immediate response to the news; then the query: "Is he still alive?"

"Affirmative."

"Kill him!"

There followed a series of coded text messages through secure channels until Scorpio reached his contact. "We have an emergency. A senior officer at Scotland Yard by the name of Harwood has received a special communication which must be retrieved and the officer neutralised."

"Understood," was the terse reply.

Harwood and Forest approached the office of Chief Superintendent Gregson apprehensively. They had had memos from the Boss Man, as he was known, but never a direct summons. A secretary ushered them inside immediately. "Please sit down" said the Chief who was sitting behind a desk- remarkably tidy Forest thought for such an important man. "I believe you received an important package?"

Harwood nodded "Yes Sir, it came today. Sergeant Forest signed for it. It's a DVD but we haven't yet had time to see what's on it." Why did Gregson visibly relax at Harwood's statement Forest wondered but said nothing. "Well now you need to know," said Gregson "that this matter has supreme significance for an ongoing investigation by Military Intelligence and I would like you, Harwood, to deliver the disc to a secure address which I will give you and, I might add, this matter falls within the Official Secrets

Act and neither of you are to divulge anything of this to anyone at all. Is that clear?" this said with commanding authority. The two police officers nodded and voiced their acknowledgement. "Right Sergeant Forest please wait outside, I've got a job for you later."

"Now Harwood, take this note on which I've scribbled the address and deliver the item as quickly as you can. The password to gain you admittance is 'Access'. Got that?"

Yes Sir" replied Harwood all too aware of his position. "And get rid of that note when you've memorised the address." Feeling mystified and irritated by Gregson's manner Harwood frowned and withdrew.

After Harwood left Sergeant Forest was called into Superintendent Gregson's office and given instructions to join a traffic operations car with a uniformed driver and proceed with immediate effect to an address in the East End where she was to serve an arrest warrant on a man wanted in connection with skipping bail.

They parked outside a rundown high rise where all the ground flats had boarded up windows. The address they wanted was situated on the third floor and although she had been led to believe that there was little likelihood of trouble she asked the driver, a young police constable called Thompson, to accompany her in view of the leering group of youths who draped the walls adjacent to the stairwell. To the accompaniment of catcalls, vocal and gestured obscenities they mounted the stairs and on the third landing stopped outside the battered and graffiti scarred doorway of number 306. Forest knocked and called out: "Police, open the door!" and held her badge up to the door spy-hole. There was a sound of bolts being drawn back and the door opened. What happened next was described by P.C. Thompson in his statement :

"Framed in the doorway stood a tall heavy set man wearing a mask and holding a sawn off shotgun which he fired point blank at Sergeant Forest who was blasted back against the railings of the landing."

Panic stricken, the young officer scrambled down the stairs and ran for his life towards the car noticing during his hysterical flight that the youths had vanished. He screamed an emergency call to H.Q. requesting an ambulance and backup. He only remembers shouting again and again

"Officer Shot, Officer Down!"

In the frenzy following the shooting the assailant vanished. Examination of the room revealed it was a bare unused place. The Forensics Officers called to the scene nodded knowingly at each other coming to an unspoken conclusion that this was a set-up. The Paramedics arrived and Sergeant Forest was pronounced dead at the scene. Superintendent Gregson ordered a full honours funeral for Forest and put out an all points search for the murderer. Constable Thompson was given counselling leave to recover. No one raised any difficult questions.

Meanwhile Harwood had requisitioned an unmarked black Vauxhall 2Lt. from the car pool and set off to make the delivery of the Disc which had been placed in a secure casing at Gregson's insistence. But as he drove along he got to thinking and questions began to form in his mind. First of all the package containing the DVD had been addressed to him personally and just how had Superintendent Gregson learned of it? Then there was the question of who was waiting at the address. And also why all the cloak and dagger fuss? With the questions came the doubts. Deciding that he needed time to think, he impulsively took the first turning on the left. As he parked alongside a dingy warehouse, a movement in the rear view mirror caught his attention. A 4 x 4 with blacked out windows was pulling into the alley and was now parked about 200 metres behind him. A creepy anxious feeling came over him and he decided to contact Sergeant Forest whose thoughtful analysis of situations he missed in circumstances like this. He tried her mobile which started to ring and then abruptly stopped. He tried again but the line was dead. Frustrated he used the in-car police radio to contact Dispatch. The woman switchboard operator answered his call immediately and after identifying himself he asked to be put through to Forest. There followed a silence at the other end as he was put on hold. After a considerable time he was connected to the Duty Desk

Sergeant who answered his request with obvious difficulty. "I'm sorry to have to tell you, Sir, but Sergeant Forest was shot and killed in the performance of her duties earlier this afternoon."

The message hit him like a blow to the head. For several moments his mind couldn't focus. He and Forest had shared years of detective work and he'd come to rely on her with absolute confidence. How could this have happened? It was beyond belief. And then he remembered Gregson saying to her "I have a job for you later." These words rang in his head with alarming overtones and then, with all the doubts, not forgetting the blacked out car parked way back behind him, his mind jumped into gear. He talked it out to himself: "This is a set-up; it is a conspiracy and somehow Forest and I have become part of it through that damned package. What will happen to me when I deliver this Disc? And why have I been told to destroy the note with the address on it?" And then with a sudden sinking feeling the awful truth dawned on him. He would be the next to die, that was his inevitable conclusion.

Harwood was an intelligent man and a clever detective. He had steady nerves and he realised that he would have to act quickly if he was to survive. He didn't know what was going on but it was damn serious. He felt frightened and alone. Time to mourn Forest later, much later. Right now he had to save his own skin. Adrenalin coursed through his body with a rush forcing him to move. Swiftly deciding on a plan of action he started the car and drove to the end of the alley. Turning right he saw that it was possible to drive further down and exit to the main road. It did not escape him that as soon as his car moved the other car followed. This sinister move only further served to confirm his suspicions.

"Well we'll see about that," he muttered to himself, feeling his anger rising and as he reached the end of the alley he slewed his car sideways so as to completely block the exit. Then grabbing the case containing the Disc and leaving the car door wide open he raced out of the lane and headed at a run for the nearest Underground Station. He knew now where he was going and what he had to do.

At Scorpio's H.Q. the alarm system was in full swing. Gregson had been called to task for his ineptitude in handling the affair but above all Scorpio among his other skills was a pragmatist, which was why his section of the network had survived many crises under his ruthless command. Now his team swung into action. Wilcox handled the task force with her usual speed and efficiency. The I.T. section began intensive surveillance of all mobile usage in the effort to locate Harwood whilst the Black Operations Combat Team were moved to armed status and Rapid Reaction mode in their stealth helicopter, ready to fly at a moment's notice.

Harwood realised intuitively that the search for him would be intensive with all the resources of the Metropolitan Police at their disposal. It grieved him considerably to think that the Force had been corrupted. Instead of heading for his flat which would be expected, he adopted a devious plan that he hoped would avoid detection. Discarding his mobile in a rubbish bin he set out to follow an escape route that he was working out as he ran.

Meanwhile Scorpio's Technology Team were busy hacking- in to world- wide satellite coverage of sections of London with the aim of tracking Harwood's whereabouts after he abandoned his car.

Harwood left the commuter line at a small station approximately 4 miles from Bromley in Kent and walked the half-mile to the cottage inherited from his grandmother which he used occasionally as a get-away. After refreshing himself with a shower and a strong coffee, he broke open the seal on the small case containing the DVD and apprehensively inserted it into the player.

What he saw shocked even him with his 20 years experience of international crime. The opening sequence showed a man aged in his mid-fifties, portly and balding with the intense look of the fanatic. Seated in an armchair in a furnished room the man began speaking to camera:-

"My name is Doctor Theo C. Adams. I am a Medical Researcher in the field of human genetics. I have worked for the last nine years for a firm who have provided me with more than adequate funding. Two months ago my research achieved the climax of all my dreams and efforts as I discovered a means of altering the genetic identity of a body by fusing it with the genetic code of another body. This exceeded all the previous research in which genetic codes could be manipulated. My results change the ways in which disease and disability can be treated. This is an astounding break through with implications that are beyond belief. The supreme product of my research, a Genetic Synthesizer, could be used to treat most diseases which are now untreatable. The application of my Synthesizer enables a superior genetic code to dominate a weaker or unhealthy code. But there is more. By the application of the Synthesizer it is possible to breach the species barrier. The significance for science is ground breaking because, for example, any two animals of different species could be combined to produce a hybrid which would incorporate the best of both. The Synthesizer accelerates the natural processes which fuel evolution by conjoining the genes of two beings into a single healthy code which has 100% survival. The resulting being is far superior to its origins and the process advances evolution by a factor of millennia to the nth. power. Naturally I expected to be free to publish my results, with patent protection, for the benefit of the world at large but my Patron Firm, which had been monitoring the progress of my work, insisted on keeping it secret. They sought to guarantee my cooperation by offering me not only great material rewards but membership of an exclusive group, a League who are aiming to infiltrate and eventually seize power in all world governments. To further persuade me to join them I was given the shattering news that the membership of the League consisted of top military personnel, including specialists in many fields of science, who were not only in contact with Alien Species from cosmic star systems but were actually working alongside these Aliens in areas of space engineering and biotechnology. I was sworn to secrecy on the pain of death if I went public on any of this information. My own research, I realised to my horror, had contributed to this criminal organisation. To instruct me in the proof for the power in the hands of this League and convert me to their cause, I was kept prisoner under guard and ordered to read the facts. Some of the evidence came from a place in the United States of America, an area simply designated as 'Area 51' that was not under that government's authority. I learned that a programme of genetic experimentation between humans and aliens to produce a new breed of hybrids had been ongoing for some of years, in which thousands of humans had been abducted by aliens for medical experimentation. But the results from using sexual mating either physical or via test tube had yielded only limited success, and merely one in 5,000 of the hybrids survived early infancy but even with these successes it proved impossible to breed from them. My original research plan which I had submitted to numerous scientific foundations had failed to attract support because it seemed too ambitious and costly but had engaged the attention of this group without question, for reasons which now became clear. The basis of my research thesis was simplicity itself. I hypothesised that just as many independent dog thoroughbreds had been developed from selective breeding of the wolf, no one had experimented with human genes to achieve changes in the breed although Nazi Germany had vainly tried to breed a super Aryan race. I called my research programme the "Wolf Research Agenda" and conducted my experiments in secrecy under the exclusive patronage of a single institution. Little did I suspect the motives of this sinister League which has in mind a super race of human and alien hybrids with the overall intention of ruling the world if not the galaxy. I was informed that an elite group, some of them human/alien hybrids already existed. Indeed I was told that the League comprised an international membership which included American, European, Russian, Chinese and Asian members. They invited me to join them as a full member. I refused and was confronted by an Alien Hybrid who operates under the code name of Scorpio. It is he who runs the League in this country and he gave me forty eight hours to decide and I then realised what would happen if I refused to join them. With exceptional luck I managed to escape, they obviously didn't think I had it in me, I copied this data on to two discs; one I gave to a journalist I had known through my previous work but she was discovered and eliminated. I saw your name in the news and hope that you can take on the responsibility of saving humanity and perhaps communicate this information to the United Nations. What I have given here is in layman's terms but in a third Disc, which I have hidden in a buried capsule, I have detailed all my research for scientific scrutiny. It may be discovered in the future by anyone investigating my death from which I fear I have no escape. I wish you much luck if you take on this task. But be warned THEY are everywhere and usually in positions of high authority."………End.

Harwood spent several moments in disbelief contemplating what he had just witnessed before experiencing a cold tingling across his scalp and down his back, a feeling bordering on terror. What chance did he have of reaching the United Nations and would they be able to tackle this League as it was called? Perhaps even the U.N. had been compromised by now. In deep thought he crossed the room to a sideboard and poured himself a stiff malt to steady his nerves. Still sipping his whiskey he climbed the narrow cottage stairs and entered what had been his grandmother's bedroom. Opening a drawer in her desk he took out a blue cotton towel which he unfolded to reveal a cleaned and oiled Army Officer Issue Webley .45 Revolver that had belonged to his father, a veteran of World War II. Also in the drawer was a silver tin in which there were eighteen cartridges carefully wrapped in cotton wool. There had been 26 but on a holiday visit some years ago he had tried out his marksmanship in a local quarry. His grandmother had refused to countenance handing in the weapon. She kept it as a treasured memento of the son who had died from the ill effects of his war wounds. Now it might come in really handy he thought; thanks Gran.

At the League HQ in London there was a flurry of intense activity as a variety of measures were set in motion to track Harwood's whereabouts. A breakthrough came with the discovery and recovery of his mobile which hadn't been turned off. C.C.T.V footage of that area identified the figure of Harwood entering a railway station serving the home counties. Satellite survey spotted their target leaving a station on the Bromley line at Pettswood. Then cloud obscured further trace but later agents on the ground elicited information from the locals at the Travellers' Rest that there was a cottage nearby where a family called Harwood used to live and "Yes, there was a grandson who was with the Police Force." "Let's make absolutely sure we get him this time." Scorpio urged his team. "But I want him alive, we need to find out what he knows!"

The Scene: The garden of Harwood's Cottage. The Time 03.00 hrs. The Sky overcast with a watery moon. Overhead: the almost silent shape of a black stealth helicopter. Soon dark shapes noiselessly descending from ropes as the League's R. and R. Force moved quickly to surround the cottage. Inside all was in darkness except for faint moonshine. The tinkling of shattered glass momentarily disturbed the inner quiet and then shadows manoeuvred down the hallway. Everywhere doors burst open and bright lights illumined the rooms. Nothing!! In the downstairs lounge the attackers found a note printed in broad felt tip pen on white paper pinned to the table. The note said:

"Foiled again. Now I'll be coming after you."

It was signed Jack Harwood. But of that person there was no trace.

"Trust no one, no one can be trusted" were the words ringing through Harwood's brain as he fled the cottage barely an hour before they came for him. He guessed that sooner or later they would trace him. After all, their resources seemed limitless and he had remembered with a curse that he'd left his mobile switched on. He assumed they'd find it and then look at C.C.T.V. footage not to mention satellite tracking which could read a newspaper from hundreds of miles up in space. He took a calculated risk and drew money out of a bank machine and then he bought some outdoor clothing an d a haversack from a sport's shop.

It took him four days of hitch hiking, mainly walking at night and cadging lifts from truck drivers, to reach the Cornish coast. He walked the narrow lanes as if he was on a hiking holiday. He was searching for a remote cove with a complement of small fishing boats and a convenient hostelry where he could bed down and consider his options. On the second day he arrived in a likely location. He stood for a while surveying the tiny harbour with its row of cottages. His trained eyes assessed the area with care and, at last, weary with travel he entered the one and only watering hole, the Smugglers Inn.

Stooping to get through the ancient door he found the inside dark and smoky. Everywhere was blackened wood that told of centuries of usage. He was aware of a momentary silence as searching eyes probed and analysed him. At the bar he enquired about the prospects for lodging from the jolly faced landlord. He was in luck as there happened to be a spare room at the back. Relaxing for the first time in days he suddenly felt hungry and again mine host was able to oblige with a tasty bar meal. Afterwards over a satisfying beer he cautiously surveyed the surroundings. Leather capped and bearded faces returned his stare but not unpleasantly. Eventually one of the company of drinkers invited him to join a corner table where a group of men in roll neck sweaters were having a rumbustious game of dominoes. After several rounds of drinks and, with his wallet somewhat lighter, he was on easy and friendly terms; he had always related easily to men like this.

Conversing with them and through gentle probing he confided that he was wanted on suspicion of smuggling tobacco and liquor. As was his plan this seemed to endear him to the happy company even more. It was then that he took a huge risk, (knowing he had to move quickly), and confided that he was looking to leave the country but didn't have his passport with him. The group registered this information without comment and after a final merry round bade him goodnight and left. Feeling tired and slightly drunk he decided that he didn't need to worry whether they would report him and flopped gratefully on his bed and slept deeply.

He awoke in terror some few hours later. A huge figure in the dark room had shaken him awake.

"We're sailing in half an hour. Settle your business and meet us outside." When his eyes were able to focus he recognised one of his companions from the night before.

"We'll not charge you for the trip but you might have to lend a hand," said with a laugh then he was gone.

Wiping the sweat from his brow Harwood checked the time, it was 3.11 a.m.

Three hours later Harwood lay below deck on a hard bunk as the boat plunged and rolled through rising seas and they left the English Channel behind them. Where he was headed he had no idea. What he was going to do he couldn't imagine. But somehow, someway he knew that he eventually would have to challenge this gigantic conspiracy. Sometime in the future there would be an opportunity for payback. Or so he fervently hoped, as the tramp witness had so blithely put it on the last normal day of his life. Meanwhile he nursed the comfortable feel of the pistol in his pocket and pondered where it might all end.

Far off among the craggy mountain peaks there came a calling in the silver moon light which echoed along the wilderness trails and rose up from deep within the river valleys and the pine forests. It was the howling of the wolf packs in lament not only for the lost litters of cubs stolen in the service of mankind but for a dawning sense that man might soon also have to mourn a loss, that of his very own humanity.

An African Adventure

There was a loud pounding and thunderous roar that was coming ever closer. All who were gathered near the waterhole stared across at the jungle. Suddenly a herd of elephants, including several calves, erupted into sight, plunged into the shallows and drank thirstily. They were a spectacular sight. After drinking their fill the leader, a large female, trumpeted a signal and they all sped off towards the trees and vanished. From arrival to departure it seemed but a brief moment but it was imprinted on my mind never to be forgotten. It was my first day at Hwange Safari Park in Zimbabwe. It was July in the African winter of 1994 and I was touring the country in the company of two married friends, Judith and Geoff. It was my first experience of Africa but they had been there before. We had hired an old but reliable Ford from a contact of Judith's and we were to share the driving.

The trip was a breath- taking episode unlike anything before in my life. The brightness of the daylight was overwhelming, wearing sunglasses was essential. The landscape glowed with a luminous quality of vivid colours so different from my home in England. On arrival I felt the air covered me in a stifling blanket of heat that had me longing for a cool shower. The alien scents made my senses reel and I was overwhelmed by the strange surroundings. I soon realised that I was wearing too many clothes and it became necessary to adopt the mandatory open necked shirt, shorts and sandals. Dinner at the Lodge that evening held a surprise for me. I was offered a menu listing crocodile and warthog for the main course. In an air of abandon I opted for crocodile which tasted remarkably like chicken. At the conclusion of the meal a grinning waiter presented me with a certificate verifying that I had indeed eaten crocodile. Afterwards I took leave of my friends who were in fact on their honeymoon to simply stand and stare at the night sky. Against a black velvet background, a myriad of dazzling stars filled the heavens like radiant diamonds. My neck ached as I strained to grasp their significance.

Sitting alone after midnight, all thoughts of bed brushed aside, I watched from behind a protective barrier, a parade of wild creatures, which I had formerly only seen in photographs or on TV. As they emerged from the surrounding jungle to slake their thirst at the lake I was stirred by their feral appearance. Whether zebra or giraffe, waterbuck or hyena, all the animals I saw emanated the natural freedom of their birthright. These animals were distinctively different from the caged zoo beasts of the so called civilised world and it showed in the confident, independent way they moved. Even a pack of jackals, red eyes reflecting the menace within, slunk stealthily out of the darkness around three am, displaying a fierce self-sufficiency. The untamed savagery I witnessed that night was an inspiring insight into the Africa of which I was now a part.

Suddenly I was joined by one of the native game wardens. His name was Joshua and he had worked at the park for the last eleven years. We shared a smoke and a small bottle of Highland Malt Whiskey I fetched from my bedroom. I cannot recall all the captivating tales of wild animals which he related to me but I do remember the excitement of an excursion we made into the interior in his Safari Jeep.

Once we had driven into the cover of the trees we could only see by the Jeep's four strong headlights supplemented by a powerful spotlight fixed to its roof. It was an exhilarating ride as we hurtled along game trails scattering the indigenous wildlife before us. It also felt claustrophobic as the jungle closed around us and we careered down a long tunnel without end. I could not name all the animals I saw that night despite the headlights for they registered simply as fleeting forms that had more to do with shadows than identifiable creatures but when we pulled into a clearing and switched off the lights all that changed. Although we could, after several moments of night blindness, see the dark bush around us, faintly illumined by starlight, we had no idea of what might be watching us. But we were soon to find out. At first there was only a hint of something bigger and blacker than the surrounding trees away to one corner. We stared apprehensively at the inky blackness at something ever so faintly silhouetted against the night from which there came disturbing sounds of rustlings, grunts and stampings. The first intimation of danger was when Joshua muttered a curse and re-started the engine. As the headlights came on I had a vision of terror. A massive bull elephant, sporting enormous angry flapping ears and long gleaming white tusks, was charging us. We had intruded into his private space and he was about to expel us with extreme prejudice. Joshua quickly crashed through the gears as we sped off, obviously he knew what I didn't, that enraged bull elephants can move very fast. I remembered feeling scared but excited at the same time. Here I was having a real African adventure just like something out of a novel by John Buchan. It was all too surreal to take in but, as we bounced and jolted along our escape route there was a huge beast behind with killing in mind. I prayed that the Jeep would not stall but thankfully we skidded and swerved our way back into the safety of the Lodge. As the ignition was switched off I looked across at Joshua and we both heaved a sigh of relief. "That was too close for comfort" he said. I agreed but had to admit, with my heart still beating wildly, that I had thoroughly enjoyed it.

Next morning I arose with the sensations of the previous night still in my mind. Mindful of the notices everywhere that cautioned us to close windows and doors securely against possible incursions by monkeys and apes, I wandered down to breakfast. The setting was an alfresco buffet and a field kitchen under a tented canopy which offered cooked breakfasts. The morning was fresh and pleasantly warm as I selected a table overlooking the lake. For starters I chose a large orange and some toast and marmalade but just as I sipped my first taste of coffee a small silver furred monkey leapt onto my table and made off with my orange. A chorus of laughter from the native chefs confirmed my opinion that visitors were regularly duped this way. Meanwhile the thief made a chirpy exhibitionist show of eating my orange from a secure perch on a baobab tree. From then on I held fast to whatever I was eating.

The rest of the day was spent touring an animal park affiliated to the Lodge. Among the experiences I had there was a close encounter with an appealing cheetah cub, just recently rescued, which growled and tried to bite me and the remarkable sight of a native worker in a fenced reptile compound feeding baby crocodiles which constantly snapped aggressively at his heels. All around me as I wandered through the park were the scents and the tastes of Africa embodied in the flowers of the hibiscus and bougainvillaea which mingled with the aroma from the eucalyptus and acacia trees.

In one section, long containers holding peanuts and seeds had been hung and a host of multi-coloured birds which I could not name zoomed around them. In another part I saw humming birds imbibing sweet juices from a bottle hung horizontally from strings. In no small measure I was enraptured by all I saw.

The afternoon was to prove no less enthralling. In a convoy of several large open sided safari trucks we sped across endless miles of savannah shimmering under the relentless burning sun. During the course of an unforgettable day I witnessed just about the whole range of African wildlife on the plains. We saw giraffes, buffalo, rhinoceros, antelope and zebra and my mind was sent in a whirl by the teeming wildlife. It had been an exhausting but rewarding day especially towards late afternoon when the air began to cool and the light diffused the landscape. Relaxing in the back of the truck I began to unwind from the exhilaration of the previous hours spent driving alongside a running mass of wild beasts. As I lay back my eyes were drawn to where sky and land seemed to blend into a panoply of colourful layers of yellow, orange and red with only the dark streaks of browsing herds to mark the horizon. It was like a large beautiful watercolour.I stored the picture in my mind to treasure for a lifetime.

After two days absorbing the natural charm of the Hwange Safari Park our small party set off in our car for Mutare, Zimbabwe's fourth largest city and the gateway to the eastern highlands. Formerly known as Umtali, 'a stream,' it was soon to figure as my favourite place and I can well understand what a popular venue it was during the days before independence when the country was known as Rhodesia. Judith had lived there for several years working at the Teachers Training College and knew the area well.

We were staying with friends of hers who rented a huge old house outside the town. I was allotted the disused servant's quarters situated in the garden which had a veranda next to a breadfruit tree. I had a pallet for sleeping and there was a shower, sink and toilet in the room. Who could ask for more? The first night we were there Judith arranged for us to meet up with some old friends at a large hut which served drinks and where people met of an evening to relax and talk. On the occasion of our visit there was a marked 'Macho' atmosphere in the place due chiefly to the presence of the local police. Tired of the laddish behaviour of the bar owner towards his female assistants, viz "Where is my drink?" Barmaid "On the desk in your office." "Why isn't it in my hand?"

As the girl hurried to retrieve his drink he beamed a superior male smirk for the benefit of those around him.

I broke away from this exhibitionist behaviour and moved along the bar to stand beside a large serious looking black man. I introduced myself and we shook hands. His name was Peter and he was the chief of the local police. We drank bottles of South African beer. He supped directly from the bottle whilst I requested a glass which he got for me. Meanwhile, the rank and file officers of his Force kept a respectful distance in a corner of the room drinking the popular opaque milky beer. We swapped stories of army experiences and then we discovered a mutual interest in handguns. I told him I was a member of my University

Gun Club where at weekends we practised marksmanship at a target range. We got along splendidly so much so that he invited me to accompany his squad on patrol the next morning. We parted good friends and he said he would call for me at eight a.m.

My English friends were horrified to learn about my new acquaintance and related tales of terror perpetrated by the Zimbabwean police. They urged me not to go with him at risk of my life. I rose early and was just finishing my mug of tea when I heard the sirens approaching. Soon a squadron of large jeeps and an armoured car squealed to a stop outside the residence and Peter, my newly-made friend of the previous evening, appeared dressed in full combat gear. He gave me a hearty hug and, grinning, said he had used the sirens to make sure I was awake. He then presented me with a pair of boots, a jacket and trousers together with a military style beret similar to his own uniform and to complete matters he gave me a gun belt and holster holding a loaded semi-automatic pistol. I dressed quickly to the accompaniment of ribald comments and laughter from the jeeps:

"Careful you don't shoot your foot off Whitey!"

I unclipped the holster and examined the pistol. It was a Browning point 9mm. semi-automatic hand gun. I checked the magazine which held eight rounds and I made a show, for the benefit of those watching, of jamming it back into the butt housing and placing the gun on safety to confirm that I knew how to handle it. As I climbed into the leading car next to Peter I caught a brief glimpse of the frightened faces of my friends and hosts at an upstairs window. I waved casually to them and smiled broadly. We sped off to the clamour of powerful engines which aroused all the dogs in the neighbourhood into a frenzy of barking and then we settled into a steady pace as our convoy streamed along towards the border with Mozambique. Peter informed me that our duty for the day was to patrol the border and to repel incursions by terrorists. It felt good to be in uniform again if only for a joy ride.

When we reached the river which marked the border Peter directed his officers to search the banksides for any traces of intrusion and he then led me to the top of a ridge overlooking a deep part of the river.

"Is this the Limpopo River?" I asked.

He gave me a serious look and without answering said gravely: "We keep the location of our border patrols secret."

"Of course" I said hurriedly. "It's the best way."

Pointing to a patch of dark water over hung by bushes about a hundred yards away he told me to watch carefully. He stooped and picked up a flat rounded stone from amongst the rubble and bending back his arm hurled it into the river. As it splashed noisily into the water a long form slid into view. Partly submerged it surged towards the location of the splash. It was a crocodile larger than any I had previously seen at the safari park. Peter said it had got so big from eating terrorists infiltrating the border from Mozambique. I guessed the enormous size of the beast to be over seven metres and Peter agreed. Staring at it lying dormant in the water like a huge log I shuddered at the thought of the menace it threatened. Peter laughed at my reaction and said that one day he would shoot it and have it stuffed for posterity but only when the cross border incidents stopped. For the moment it was more of a deterrent than any police patrol although he did mention that one time on a night patrol they had fired upon a group attempting to swim across and then heard the thrashing and screams as the croc attacked the wounded. I managed a sickly smile and gulped uneasily at the image of what must have happened.

Suddenly there was the sound of gunfire. Peter ran to his jeep and grabbed a small machine gun, a Hechler-Koche with a telescopic laser sight. Obviously the Police Department didn't stint on the quality of their weapons I thought to myself.

"Leave the shooting to me unless you need to!" he said. Obviously I had been given the gun simply as a goodwill gesture in relation to our conversation of the previous night. It wouldn't look good on report for a tourist to be involved in a shooting.

When we reached the others it turned out to be a false alarm. One of the men thought he had seen movement in the bushes across stream and opened fire with his Kalishnikov rifle but it turned out to be only a group of foraging baboons who escaped unscathed.

"Lucky for the Baboons" I said and Peter laughed and added by way of explanation: "Our rules of engagement with terrorists are simple. We shoot on sight and we shoot to kill."

"I'll try to remember that" I said with a smile as I returned my pistol to its holster. I worried about the implication that no attempt was made to distinguish between a refugee and a terrorist but thought it best to say nothing.

Later we stopped at a wayside café and ordered sandwiches for lunch. Afterwards I bought a round of drinks for the small squad and answered a lot of questions about England. Information about Zimbabwe was muted and many of my casual queries went unanswered.

The squad delivered me to my residence just as it was turning dark. Convivial handshakes were exchanged and I was left with an impression of camaraderie especially from Peter. We made vague promises to meet again and I quickly changed back into my holiday togs and handed all the equipment back. Despite a few things that had disturbed me I had enjoyed the day and found Peter and his men refreshing company after being restricted to the companionship of my friends who were, to say the least, of a sedate disposition. But when I thought about the emotional vibrations during the course of the day I felt that I had been part of something sinister.

My friends and host made little mention of my escapade and the following day we departed for the Eastern Highlands where we were booked into chalets which had formerly been part of a tea plantation near Chipinge. On arrival we were served cocktails on the veranda of the reception area which offered picturesque views of the distant mountains, one of which had an unusual conical shape. I pointed to it and asked its name but none of the staff were able to give me an answer. I also noted something strange about their responses to my question, it was as if the subject was taboo. Since it was still quite early in the afternoon I decided, after having a bath and a shave, to take a walk in the countryside. The place was enclosed by a fenced and gated compound and as I walked out the gatekeeper, whom I gathered doubled as caretaker and general factotum, became quite worried and advised me not to go. When I asked for reasons he just rolled his eyes and said:

"Don't go Sah. Bad mountain spirits get you and eat you up!"

Although inwardly I scoffed at his warning and assured him that I wouldn't go far, it was not the first time I'd heard such superstitious tales. Dismissing it as simply a part of ingrained African culture I set out to explore the immediate vicinity of the old plantation. I carried a strong ebony stick which I'd bought at a Flea Market in Johannasburg and which was etched with mystical carvings which, I had been told, by the native stall holder, would protect me from evil spirits. I had been striding out for about twenty minutes when I had an uncanny feeling that I was lost and glancing around worriedly I realised that I was not sure of my bearings. Just then, to aggravate matters further, it grew dark. Actually it was not a gradual process, it happened all at once. One second it seemed I was standing in daylight and the next I was encircled by impenetrable darkness. As the saying goes: "It was pitch black."

I couldn't see my hand in front of me. I became aware of minute disturbing sounds round about and I felt a chill wind stirring the air. My imagination went into over drive and fear took hold of me. I didn't dare move. All at once I heard a man shouting. I yelled back in return and then increasingly I became aware of someone calling: "Where are you Sah!"

It was the gatekeeper and I began to see in the distance a light. Alerted by my cries the light moved in my direction until I could see him coming holding a burning torch aloft. My relief was visceral. We hastened back to the compound together and once safely inside I hugged my rescuer in relief and thanked him profusely. I learned that his name was Jacob and that he originally came from Bulawayo. I offered him a large tip for his services which he at first declined but I insisted. After all the man could well have saved my life by his rescue action. As we parted he reminded me: "Remember

Sah, dark come down pretty damn quick here and then dem demons come looking.

Dinner was either warthog stew with spiced rice or herb omelette. I had the stew which was remarkably tasty much to the distaste of my friends who tended to eat only vegetarian food. Fortunately my latest venture had escaped their notice so I didn't have to explain anything. I was still quite traumatised by my walk on the wild side and was glad to find there was a bar available. After a few stiff drinks I had managed to mentally transform my recent adventure into a macho Hemmingway type experience in my mind at least.

Around midnight and, after bidding everyone goodnight, I headed straight for my chalet and bed but it was not to be. On going into the bathroom I suddenly realised that I was not alone. I turned to see the wriggling shape of a large snake in the bathtub. The sight terrified me and made the hairs on the back of my neck stand up. It was trying to get out of the bath but was having difficulty climbing the slippery sides. It must have been after water and got stuck. As I moved towards the door keeping a wary eye on it, the snake rose up and began hissing. I slipped out and slammed the door shut. I was astonished at finding the snake in the room because I had taken extra care to check that the windows were shut and the door locked before I went to dinner. Breathing heavily I leaned against the door and wondered what on earth I could do. The snake was quite a size and I judged it was likely to be deadly venomous. I could spend the night with the bathroom door closed but on looking down I saw with dismay that there was an appreciable gap at the bottom of the door which would provide ease of access for a snake. By this time all the lights in the compound had been turned off and the thought of going out there and encountering whatever might be slithering about was anathema to me. I could hear no sounds at all and so concluded that no one was about. Then I had an idea. Perhaps if I shouted for help my vigilant friend, the security guard at the gate, would hear me and come to my aid. Cautiously I eased the steel frame window in the bedroom open a fraction and placing my face in the gap I yelled for help. I continued yelling until I grew hoarse with the effort. No one responded, no one came. I closed the window and sat on the bed. Whatever needed doing would have to be done by myself alone.

I decided to get fully dressed despite the heat. Donning a roll neck sweater and long trousers and wearing leather shoes on my feet I tucked my trouser ends into a pair of thick socks. In this way I hoped to protect my body if the snake attacked me. I searched the room looking for something to use as a weapon. In a slim cupboard I found a thick mop with a long handle. It would have to do. Wrapping one of my own hand towels around my left hand and extending the mop before me, I quickly entered the bathroom. The snake was still in the bath and reared up as I approached. I charged forward and pinned the snake against the side of the bath with the mop head. Holding it there firmly I turned on the two taps next to my end of the room. The snake put up a really strong fight, wriggling and darting around the bath which was fast filling with water. I kept sloshing the mop around the snake's body as it thrashed about. Then an idea came to me as I fought the snake, I would attempt to drown it. I turned both taps full on. Since there was no plug in the outlet the bath did not overflow but the room gradually began to fill with steam. I carried on pushing the snake under the hot water. At one point it managed to jerk its head free and spat a spray of spit which missed me and then I pushed it under the steaming water again. I don't know how long the fight lasted but after a while I sensed that the snake was weakening and I was able to trap the creature in a corner of the bath and hold its head under the mop. Eventually I could see that it had ceased to move and was probably dead or dying. I maintained the pressure on it for a long time until I was full satisfied that it was finished. At last I relaxed my hold with the mop and was relieved to see that the reptile's body simply floated partly submerged. I was soaked with sweat from my efforts and the thick steam from the hot water. I turned off the taps and allowed the bath to drain. The snake's body lay inert on the bottom of the bath. I grabbed a large towel from the rail and wrapping it around the body I carried it into the bedroom, opened the door to the outside and threw it away, towel and all.

Then I poured myself a large whiskey and sat on the bed. It was now after two o'clock. I had been fighting that thing for almost three hours. I found that I was shaking and my nerves felt as if they were on a raw edge. I hated the idea of having to kill anything but if I'd been bitten the snake would have killed me I felt sure. God only knows where the nearest hospital was and then there would have been the problem of getting me there. I was mystified as to how the snake had got into my room in the first place but then Africa was full of surprises and the wild life tended to be up close and dangerous.

I sat up with the light on all night occasionally dozing but not sleeping. Come morning I heard one of the staff sweeping the paths outside muttering as he picked up the towel. There followed a mixture of a scream and a shout as the snake's body was uncovered. Another worker joined the first and I heard them exclaiming "Green Mamba, Green Mamba," in shocked tones.

After eating a welcome breakfast and giving my account of the events of the night to my friends who were scared stiff by my story, I walked around the garden areas to clear my mind and get my emotions into balance. The gatekeeper, having heard of my nightmare experience, sought me out.

"You lucky man, Sah. Dem damned spirits done send you a bad thing. Don't go anywhere outside, boss. They catch you quick. You been get warning."

I thanked him for his advice and I was just unnerved enough by the night's events to believe that he could be right. I felt truly like an innocent abroad. He added that one bite of the Green Mamba would have killed me. "Pretty damned quick!"

But what truly perplexed me was how did the snake get into my locked and closed room?

I spent the day reading to keep my mind off thinking about dark spirits and black African magic. I took Jacob's advice and did not venture forth from the compound. In the afternoon I strolled around inside and discovered a pond where some exotically coloured ducks were swimming. Above the pond there was a high tree festooned and wrapped around with vines and foliage. A movement in the tree top caught my attention and as I watched a big spider emerged and began weaving tangled strands to its already large web. I made a speedy retreat. This creepy place was beginning to totally unnerve me. Thank goodness we were due to leave the next day.

We drove north towards the Zambian border, our destination was Victoria Falls. As the road surmounted the plateau which led to the border area we stopped to take in the view. As soon as the car engine was switched off and we got out of the car we could hear the roar of the water over the falls. The view in the direction of the sound was breath taking. A wall of mist like a translucent veil hung over the location. Sunlight was dimmed to a glow through a film of watery haze which later, as we walked through the rain forest park, felt moist on the skin and cooled the air and I felt as if I was seeing the world through a boundless glazed membrane. The sight of the vast amount of water cascading over the falls was magnificent and riveting. Engrossed by the spectacle I made my way as close as I could get to see the chasm into which the water was crashing when I was confronted by two armed policemen standing in front of a roped off area. Apparently it was not unknown for people bent on committing suicide to jump over the side and I learned later that, a few days before our visit, a clergy woman intent on taking photographs had stepped over the rope in an unguarded moment, slipped on the wet surface and slid over the edge. The immensity of the impression gained by simply standing and looking at the falls was overwhelming and rather frightening. It was yet again, I thought, an episode of Africa at its most awe inspiring.

We stayed for two remarkable days before heading south to Bulawayo where we stayed with a friend of Judith's. Her husband was a native of Zimbabwe and held the rank of colonel in the army. He was at pains to show me a polished shell casing the like of which had killed many of his comrades in the war of independence. Their house, like many in the country, was enclosed by a steel perimeter fence and guarded by four large dogs one of which, a German Shepherd, took a strong dislike to me and had to be restrained in my presence.

The next morning I availed myself of the opportunity to visit the cricket ground where England had played many Test Matches against the national home team and was pleased to see how well maintained it was. The sport of cricket hade a long and illustrious tradition in Zimbabwe dating back to the days when it was Rhodesia. I remember the lady of the house, Barbara by name, offering us green and yellow striped caterpillar pods to eat, a local delicacy, which I politely refused. Crocodile and Warthog I would try but bug- like creatures had no appeal.

After leaving Bulawayo we headed back for Mutare which was in the throes of a national celebration called Heroes Day. On the way into the town we were stopped repeatedly at army checkpoints where we had to show our passports. There was also a formidable police presence and I looked out for Peter and his squad but there was no sign of them. The reason for the excessive security was that the President, Robert Mugabe, was due to visit the area the following day. On reaching the outskirts of the town we were stopped yet again and this time we had to exit the car which was thoroughly searched and we were subjected to detailed questioning. During our interrogation I observed a soldier wearing colonel insignia standing apart from the armed soldiers surrounding us. His stance was swaggering and his face wore a tight smile but his eyes were full of menace. I feared what would happen if we made the slightest wrong move. Strange to see how a smile can veil a threat. Eventually we were waved on and were relieved to be reunited with our hosts, Jean and John, once more.

The next morning after breakfast I walked down to the main street of the town, Herbert Chitepo Way. There were armed soldiers everywhere lining the streets and traffic was at a standstill. A crowd of onlookers was gathering and the arrival of the president was expected soon. After an hour standing in the hot sunlight I was about to leave when there was an unearthly clattering of engine noise and three helicopter gunships loomed overhead. It was understood that President Mugabe was in one of them. They zoomed away to land nearby and then we heard the wailing siren of a special ambulance which was the President's preferred form of transport wherever he visited or so I was told by a person in the crowd. The ambulance whisked him away to address a meeting of his supporters. I slipped into a gift shop which had a coffee counter to escape the sun and watched everything through the window. After a while the whole proceedings were played out in reverse and after the departure of the President's gunships the soldiers dispersed and the crowd withdrew.

Later that evening I went walkabout through the town. My friends were visiting their old acquaintances and I liked to wander through unfamiliar places. Outside the bank I met Johnson who was on guard. He was carrying a .303 Lee

Enfield Rifle which I recognised from my National Service in the British Army. He was anxious for company and as we talked it transpired that he had received no firearms training and possessed no ammunition. He allowed me to inspect his rifle which was so rusted and dirty that it was unfit for purpose. Obviously it was only for show and I worried for him. I advised him if attacked to use the gun as a club. He was a cheerful man and I enjoyed our conversation.

Later I came in contact with another security guard called William who had two large dogs with him. He was on patrol around the department stores and said that if he suspected anything he simply opened the ground floor door and sent in the dogs which were trained to capture intruders. He had made several arrests this way. He was married and had two young sons. We swapped niceties for a while. A spiv like character began following and pestering me for money. When William noticed this as he did his rounds he joined me again and chased him off. As I returned to my lodging I felt that I had made two friends that evening.

The following morning I was again on my own and headed down town to buy an international newspaper which was printed in English. On my way my attention was caught by a procession of people led by a man in a white robe in the grounds of a large house. They stopped in front of a huge tree and on the fringe of the gathering I spotted a person I'd met at a social gathering recently. He recognised me and beckoned me to join him. In response to my questions

Wild Adventures in Time and Place

he informed me that the meeting was to conduct a blessing on the spirit of the tree which had been causing havoc in the house much to the distress of the family. Aware of my curious stare he stated that this was the way problems were managed here and bade me watch quietly. The holy man in white performed a ritual by the tree and then turned to those gathered before him. A man and a woman stepped forward and each proffered a bottle of something. The pastor took each bottle and emptied it around the base of the tree whilst making an incantation. After which the small group nearest joined him in what I surmised to be a communal prayer. I turned to my companion and asked what was in the bottles. "Gin, to libate the spirit" he said as if it was the most normal thing in the world to pour at least a litre of gin over a tree. I thanked him for the experience and we went our separate ways.

I headed for a little café which cooked excellent omelettes infused with herbs. I determined that I would in the next few days check out that tree because in my estimation alcohol would kill it. Each day during the remainder of my stay I checked that tree and not only did it live, it flourished.

I was invited to an evening soiree at the Teacher's College where Judith had previously taught. At the party I met up again with my companion from the tree ceremony. I told him how healthy the tree looked and he confirmed my findings and further mentioned that the trouble in the house had ceased after the ritual with the gin. I then took the opportunity to question him about something that was of keen interest to me. I asked him if he knew where I could contact a witch doctor. He gave me a really serious look at that and asked the reason for my request. I explained that as a professional psychologist I was interested in the powers of the mind and that I assumed that was also the province of witch doctors. He said that he would be in touch. The next morning he called at my chalet and said that if I was serious about my request of last night I should follow him but not on the same side of the road. He would stop to tie a shoe lace when he was opposite the house where a witch doctor practised his craft. I followed him down the main road into Mutare and sure enough he gave me the signal when I stood outside a large stone colonial type house. Quite excited at the prospect of meeting a character I had only read about I ventured up the drive and knocked at the front door. I could hear footsteps advancing down the hall and the door opened to reveal a medium sized black man smiling broadly.

"Come in my friend" he said "I have been expecting you!"

He ushered me into the hall and along to a room where a young woman and two small children were having tea. He introduced them as his daughter and his grandchildren. I told him my name and said that I was an Englishman visiting the country and perhaps he had mistaken me for someone he was expecting.

"Not a bit of it" he assured me in perfect English "I have known that you were coming for several days now. You are most welcome and I know why you are here."

I was served a cup of aromatic tea and a slice of ginger cake. We talked amicably whilst the children played and then he invited me to follow him upstairs where he led me into a room empty of furniture except for a large rush mat. The walls were decorated with African native art such as sculptures of wooden heads and paintings of wildlife. He told me to squat down by the mat and he left the room. When he reappeared he wore a genuine looking leopard skin and also a coloured head dress of feathers. On his arms and ankles he was wearing what I took to be various amulets. As he entered the room he brought with him something akin to darkness only it wasn't darkness it was a kind of other worldly light that dominated the room. He squatted opposite me and from inside his garment he produced a wooden bowl and five dried and hardened berries which he scattered on the floor between us. He then took from a pocket in his leopard skin some small black items that had the appearance of the bones of birds or tiny animals. He commenced to shake these in the bowl and then he scattered them on the mat in front of me beside the berries. He closed his eyes and began to sway from side to side and mutter sounds which were meaningless to me. He suddenly opened his eyes and began speaking to me in a high pitched voice as if he was in a trance. At this stage I was starting to feel nervous but what he told me proved to be one hundred percent accurate and was very private and personal. One thing he mentioned was a revelation to me but I realised the truth of it immediately. He said that someone in my social circle was extremely jealous and hateful of me and had consulted through Indian friends a shaman who had placed a curse on me. At this juncture my heart beat wildly because I knew who this person was and that she had many Indian acquaintances. He instructed me as to what to do when I got home, a simple ritual to rid myself of any residual effects of this curse. He also said that he would send them a warning to leave me alone.

I told him of my trauma at the Tea Plantation. He smiled and said that the Eastern Highlands was a mysterious region where dark spiritual forces abounded and it was best to avoid going into the area without adequate protection I thanked him and paid him his fee of a paltry few Zimbabwean dollars and we parted in a most friendly manner. We exchanged addresses and he gave me the phone number of his daughter's work place in a travel shop. He asked me to write and tell him if his forecast for my future materialised as he predicted and I agreed to do so. I felt truly uplifted by this experience in a way I had never envisaged. He asked me not to broadcast his name around since the authorities frowned on witchcraft practices; the old ways are not in fashion but are desperately needed all the same he told me. I reflected at this point that what I had just experienced had little or nothing to do with the scientific psychology I practised. Then he inquired about the colour of the person who had directed me to him and appeared much relieved to know he was black.

I was sad to leave Mutare, it seemed a place where I'd be happy to live for the rest of my life. We drove all day to reach the capital Harare where we were yet again to stay with former friends of Judith. Maureen and Lincoln lived in a grand house situated in its own fenced compound with a sliding door electric gate. They had two young boys and both had University degrees from Britain. A young married couple lived on site in their own accommodation and did some cooking and general housework. We brought traditional gifts of food and English magazines and some toys for the children. During our stay there for the few days before flying home I did the round of urban shops and bought two silk shirts that took my fancy and a lucky charm, a small figurine of a striped Zimbabwean cat with an extra long tail. But that first night I was in for a shock. Maureen was an excellent hostess and cooked a superb meal. After dinner we talked the evening away and I was the last to go to bed. My sleeping quarters were an improvised bed in the study and the moment I entered the room I recoiled. As I switched on the light there were sudden movements on the wall above my bed by the half open fanlight window. Two enormous black tarantula type spiders and two smaller long legged ones were grouped together.

"No way!" I said to myself "am I going to sleep beneath those things. What if they should drop on me during the night?" I resolved to try and chase them out the window if I could and began a search of the house for some implement to use. A furtive search revealed nothing of use because all the brooms and mops were kept in the servant's quarters however I did find some old newspapers. That would have to suffice. Rolling up two together I determined to be up and at them. But as I flailed and thrashed at them, the huge spiders simply moved out of my way. As my efforts became more frantic I must have been making a great deal of noise and the door suddenly swung open to present the whole family, including my friends Geoff and Judith, aghast at what was going on. Then everyone was at pains to tell me that the spiders would do me no harm and that their sole purpose was to deal with any mosquitos which might bring malaria into the house. I was truly mortified but after everyone went back to bed I still could not bring myself to sleep in the same room as those things. Therefore I spent the night sleeping in a chair in the sitting room with the lights on.

However we spent a happy week with the family in Harare. Following my 'Spider Nightmare' the servants cleared my bedroom of the creatures and closed the window so that I was able to sleep peacefully in there for the remainder of my stay.

Wild Adventures in Time and Place

It was interesting but shocking to hear of Maureen's experiences when she was studying in England. Apparently at the time the presence of a black African student was unusual and at first they treated her as an oddity and asked her ridiculous questions such as whether she slept in a tree when she was back home and did she eat only leaves and fruit. Later, as they got to know her better, she made some very good friends. Lincoln also had his share of amusing stories from his student days in England when he was at first regarded as some kind of 'Tarzan of the Apes.' One day when we were having a long conversation, Lincoln did point out for my benefit life in Africa was very different from English culture. I had mentioned to him my occult contacts with supernatural phenomena and this seemed to give him the opportunity to further enlighten me on this subject. He illuminated me on many things in relation to how different life was in East Africa compared to England. He referred to the work of Charles Darwin who suggested that Africa was the 'Cradle of Life.' Lincoln said that for him it rightly implied that his country was a fertile source of 'Life Power' which could take many forms. He said that when gin was poured onto the roots of a tree, as I had witnessed, it was meant as a gift of respect for the spirit of the tree which would consume it. The gin was for the spirit not the tree. Just as when the machinery in a waterworks was disrupted, it was a spiritual rather than a technical problem and meant that the 'Beings' of the water, he called them 'Mermaids,' needed to be placated before normal functioning would resume. He told me that sometimes these water spirits took children hostage. They would disappear presumed drowned, and reappear some days later having been 'Educated' or absorbed by African culture which was their heritage. He spoke in all sincerity and in a most genuine way. I was bewildered by what he said but I had to respect the intelligence and wisdom of this man who was not only educated to Western European university standards but came from a long line of tribal chiefs and was certainly no fool.

In their enclosure Maureen and Lincoln had a bathing pool. It was empty because it was wintertime but with temperatures in the twenty celsius range we found the days very hot. To satisfy us Lincoln and Maureen filled the pool and Judith and I had a great afternoon swimming and luxuriating in the water whilst the sun blazed down on us. The comedy of the situation was impressed upon me by the presence of the entire family, clad in sweaters and anoraks standing by the side of the pool watching us in amazement.

All too soon it seemed it was time to return home. After a day's further shopping in Harare, we said our goodbyes and flew to Johannesburg for a one night stay. In the evening I was preparing to embark on my usual walkabout when the Hotel staff cautioned me against leaving the security of the hotel. In no uncertain terms they informed me of the dangers to visitors due to the high crime rate. The manager put it rather bluntly: "You go out on the town tonight and you won't come back!"

Accepting their warning I watched a re-run of a South Africa versus England cricket test match on TV and went to bed early. The next day we boarded a South African Airways Boeing 747 for Heathrow England. On take-off as I watched the verdant landscape slide beneath us I knew that nothing would surpass let alone equal my African experience. It had truly been an adventure, it had also been an education.

The Life of A National Serviceman
An Army life Memoir

It was a far far better feeling to savour that fine autumn day, travelling along railtracks that wound through tree-lined banks steeped in wild flowers, than to arrive at my destination in Aldershot. The arrival ushered in a beginning of horrendous proportions for the next two years. The passage for me to an adult life would bear many overtones of my childhood by way of physical and emotional challenges to my selfhood. Joining the army as a National Serviceman at eighteen years of age proved to be a case of 'Out of the frying pan and into the fire.' It seemed that my early life of repression and hardship was just a 'Taste' of what I could expect in the army.

My train stopped at a special army embarkation station outside Aldershot and I joined a crowd of young men lining up on a huge square. Sergeants with name lists assigned each of us to one of four army buses. My name was called for Bus No. 4 which took us to Blenheim Barracks. On the bus I sat next to a lad called Harry who had failed to achieve a place at Leeds University to study Physics and hence was called up to serve. Under instructions we all filed into a large canteen and were given a mug of sweet milky tea and a currant bun. The tea tasted awful and was mostly wasted on us except that we were all thirsty and needed a drink of some sort.

Someone on the table where I was sitting said "They put Bromide in it." A chorus of "What's that for?" questions followed bringing the sobering reply "It's meant to make us easier to control." "But that sort of thing is not allowed, is it?" "Can they do that?"

"The Army can do what it likes." "It's what the government want." "They've got us by the balls!"

Suddenly loudspeakers in the room blared out a message. Teatime was over and we were all directed to assemble outside. When we'd lined up we were marched to an enormous building that looked like an aircraft hangar. Once inside we were formed into circles and told to remove all our clothing. Several men broke ranks in panic and made a dash back for the exit. It was basic animal behaviour motivated by an instinct for freedom and survival. Military Police, formidable looking soldiers wearing red caps, white belts and gaiters, blocked their way and several scuffles erupted. The runaways were quickly subdued and handcuffed to a metal bar which was attached to the wall all around the hall. The Army obviously were prepared for any eventuality. Several of the restrained men began to bawl and pulled despairingly at the handcuffs which caused a rush of tears in lots of eyes. The effects of witnessing this scenario was not lost on us. Everyone was tense and fearful of what might be about to happen. At this point a senior looking soldier wearing elaborate badges of rank stood up on a stage and addressed the assembly.

"You are all here enlisted by government law for National Service and it is the purpose of Her Majesty's Army to make soldiers of you so that you can serve your country during the next two years. Please be well advised to accept that your life as a civilian with all its rights and privileges is withdrawn for the present and you are now under martial law. We encourage you to make the best of and learn the most from your army service. So do your utmost to be a real benefit to the army and to yourselves."

As the lines of young men slowly undressed in the cold hall, uniformed soldiers passed around sheets of brown paper, pieces of string and Biro pens so that our civilian gear could be packaged and posted back to our homes in 'Civvy Street.'

A further terse announcement caused a stir among the near naked ranks of men.

"Anyone having problems removing his underpants should raise a hand and a Sergeant will come and cut them off for you." There ensued a flurry of activity among the few remaining men who needed to divest themselves of the ultimate underwear. The atmosphere in the hangar already taut with emotion grew increasingly strained as men, unused to public displays of nakedness, protectively covered their genitals with nervous hands and looked around fearfully. I caught the eye of a jovial looking man who smiled and shrugged as if to say "What can we do about all this?" I smiled back but didn't really feel like smiling. What was happening could be either viewed as a hilarious farce, in which case it could be laughed off and used for jokes or as ruthless subjugation causing men to submit to be absorbed into a new regime. Recruits were in a 'No Win' situation because the army held the upper hand whatever the reaction of the recruits might be. A joker said "Well it can't be as bad as the French Foreign Legion." Another wit retorted "I wouldn't be so sure about that" which caused a trickle of humour across the lines of naked bodies struggling to pack their parcels.

Stripped of clothing, cut off from family and friends and facing an apparently hostile unknown future, we recruits were deigned to submit to the process of being born again as soldiers of the Queen. Shivering with the cold under that huge dome, we filed in line to be equipped with basic army regulation clothing from the skin out. In no time at all we were given a new identity and, after our heads were shaven by a barber waiting at the end of the assembled line, a new appearance, with which to face the world.

It was early evening by the time we were fully kitted out with work clothes, known as fatigues, and with a mattress and bedding. By this time I was becoming increasingly convinced of the army's duplicity in manipulating us and so when it appeared that tall men were issued with smaller sizes and shorter men with extra large outfits my conviction that our self- esteem was undergoing a bashing was confirmed. We were next assigned to billets in Nissen huts which each housed eighteen recruits with one Corporal in a separate room. In the hut assigned to my group we made up our beds in the strained silence that shock induces. The Corporal in charge advised us to use the washroom and undress for bed as quickly as we could since it was 'Lights out' in ten minutes. "Reveille, he said, will be five thirty am followed by an outdoor physical exercise session before breakfast."

In the oppressive darkness of that long room eighteen men struggled to come to terms with the start of a new life. There was little sleep for most of us and there was much blubbering of self- pity into pillows. All too soon we were being roused in the harsh glare of lights and the bedlam of banging and shouting. Amid bellowed commands intended to rouse us we hastily dressed in the regulation shorts and singlets provided and filed out into the chilly morning air to do aerobic exercises at a pace which stretched the capacity of most of us and tempered our endurance. Feeling sick with exhaustion we staggered into the cookhouse to be offered a breakfast of fried potatoes and cheese and the ubiquitous army tea. The smell of the fried cheese induced instant nausea and sickly disbelief which were the impressions mostly registering on the faces in the queue for food. I looked across the table at men whose eyes expressed the trauma of separation from the life they had known almost as if they had been given a prison sentence. There was much furtive looking in wallets at photographs of loved ones back at home. Anything that would ease the present anguish.

Wild Adventures in Time and Place

"I really miss my dog" a sandy haired fellow with a ready smile sitting opposite confided. I nodded sympathetically but since I carried no comfort photographs nor did I have a dog to pine for, I had only my own mind as a resource on which to depend. In the midst of this nostalgia I also needed something to alleviate the stark suffering of the present. For me it was a precious memory to which I could go at will. I first became aware of these 'nutshell' gems of experience, I call them 'Emotional lifeboats,' when I first read Shakespeare at grammar school. One of my favourites is from the Tempest:

"Where the bee sucks there suck I,

In a cowslip's bell I lie

There I couch when owls do cry."

These words conjure up a place in the imagination to which a person can escape when stressed. I had a collection of such nutshells.

On that morning in that grim army barracks I turned my mind away from the present and escaped into a favoured memory of my experiences watching wildlife in the woods near my home as a boy.

Such precious moments, couched in a pocket of time, were to be forever savoured as comforts, and these images enable us to escape stressful moments and return to reality refreshed by the emotional uplift they afford. Their function is to protect and preserve our sanity during times of adversity.

They were much needed during those early days of training whilst the army was knocking us into shape. 'Square Bashing,' that is learning to march in formation and obey the various drill commands, was a physically exhausting business in which personal sensitivities were often deliberately abused and blatantly outraged. One Corporal drill instructor obviously harboured animosities towards the 'Irish' and made a point of targeting me.

"O'Connor, are you English?"

"Yes Corporal" I replied.

"I don't believe you. You're a liar just like the rest of that scruffy, shiftless bog crazy religious lot. Well, I'll be watching you and you'd better come up to English standards or I'll see you in the stockade, (The Camp Prison)."

Thereafter he took every opportunity to humiliate and find me wanting. At least my childhood had inured me against such treatment. Other men came in for similar torments which were all part of breaking us down and putting us back together Army style. It was cruel and it was viciously sadistic but it was the 'Norm' in the training to which we were subjected.

After a while it failed to have any impact on us, we were 'Roughened' as it were and the 'Tough Guy' posturing that went with such treatment served only to reveal the depths to which human interactions could sink. The NCOs responsible for training were hard, uncouth, uncultured men, the salt of the earth as General Kitchener called them.

Abstract concepts such as Truth and Honour and the Noble Warrior of Greek Classical literary tradition were none existent concepts here.

After nine weeks of hard initial training everyone in the squad was looking forward to Christmas leave when the Sergeant dropped a bombshell. The whole of the October Intake was paraded out on the square whilst he strutted in front of us wearing a broad smirk as he delivered the devastating news.

"All of you will no doubt be looking to getting Christmas leave passes for the holidays. Well there are conditions attached since the Company requires guards and men for cookhouse duties over the holidays and so we have organised a five mile run for you and the last sixty men to complete the run will be providing duties here over the Christmas and New Year."

A collective groan spread like a wave through the ranks. But there was worse to come.

"And just to make things a little bit harder for you" he grinned wickedly "You'll be running in full kit just like Napoleon and Wellington's troops did. That is all."

I had admit to feeling queasy after the news because my experience of running was in the two twenty yard sprints on school sports day. I doubted whether I could even finish a five mile hike through the fields and woods in December but in full kit? Whilst I was not overly anxious to be at home over the holiday I was looking forward to seeing my grandmother and Uncle John. Also it would be a blessed release to escape this place for a few days.

That evening I was on cookhouse fatigues which added to my depression. Scrubbing large pans free of burnt food and grease did nothing to raise the spirits and after that the cookhouse floor had to be polished clean and so I knew I would be lucky to be free until after midnight. In the midst of wiping dirty dishes from a pile which seemed never ending I felt a nudge from the man next to me.

"Don't let what that fucking little Hitler said this morning worry you. I'll see you finish the run in good time, alright! Just leave it to me."

His name was John McKay but he always went by the name 'Jock.' He slept in the next bed to mine. One night in the billet he'd run out of cigarettes and was desperate for a smoke. I let him have a packet of ten Woodbines I had spare because I hardly smoked at all. Since then he'd adopted me as a buddy especially since I'd helped him write a letter home to his girl friend, a lass called Sheilis. He was a giant of a man compared to me, being well over six foot tall and broad with it. Even though we were about the same age it was as if we were from a different race. On the first night of our service I had noticed him sitting up in bed wearing a string vest, a tam-o'-shanter on his head and reading a girlie magazine. A young Lance corporal walking up and down the aisle stopped at Jock's bed and ordered him to get rid of 'That filthy magazine and take your funny hat off.' At this Jock dropped the magazine in front of him, glared at the Corporal and reached back under his pillow to extract a sheath knife. In full view he drew a long bladed vicious-looking knife and commenced to stroke the side of his cheek with it, not uttering a word. The Corporal actually blushed, turned aside and walked on without further comment.

"How did you manage to keep that out of sight this afternoon?" I asked in surprise.

Jock turned to me with a leering grin and gave a broad wink:

"Easy. Aah just sat doon on it 'til aall the fuss was over."

The incident made me wonder how many strange bedfellows I was sleeping alongside but Jock proved to be a warm and amusing friend. He told me tales of a life very different from my own. His home was in a tenement block area of Glasgow called the Gorbals which was dominated by petty criminals and rodents and he told me it was routine to always wear boots and stamp your feet when leaving the flat in case there were rats on the stairs. For stealing and fighting he'd spent several periods in a young offenders institution ever since the age of thirteen and latterly he'd been advised by the Probationary Authorities to make the Army his career. In the light of rules to the contrary we became firm friends and spent our rest periods together talking and drinking light beer in the N.A.A.F.I. cafe. I noticed that the Corporals tended to give Jock a wide berth.

One Saturday night we had a pass to go down into Aldershot and later, after a trip to the cinema, we were having a quiet drink upstairs in the Servicemens' Club when a fight broke out below and furniture was thrown about and smashed. We couldn't leave the building without going down stairs but from the windows we saw that the military police had been summoned and were arriving in force.

"They'll arrest us if we stay here" Jock said "Nobody gets away without a beating from those buggers." With this he picked up a steel table and smashed it though a large plate glass window fronting onto the backstreet. Clearing away the shards of glass he yelled at me to follow him as he negotiated a flat roof and slid down the side into an alley. "Come on, kid!" he shouted and caught me as I leapt down from the roof. Suddenly from around a corner a military policeman appeared waving his long stick baton. "Stop you two! You're under arrest."

Jock reacted with lighting speed, obviously born of experience. He lunged forward and grabbed the policeman by the shoulders, head butted him twice and then clubbed him to the ground. He then proceeded to kick him in the ribs and groin several times. "He'll no be arresting anybody for a wee while." I was amazed at Jock's rapid reaction to the incident which was over in seconds. "C'mon kid, run like hell!" he roared at me." We fled along backstreets until we were clear of the mob and made our way safely back to barracks. I worried about the episode with the military policeman but to my relief nothing further was heard.

***

It appeared that most of the men that were billeted with me were illiterate or semi-illiterate as was pointed out to me by the Personnel Officer when he interviewed me. He was perplexed as to why, with my qualifications, I had been included in this batch. He queried why I had not joined the Territorial Army Officer Training Corps at school and I was at pains to tell him that I had spent most of my spare time playing cricket. He put me down for Officer Training but said that I'd have to do a clerk's course first. He said that I'd be posted out early in the New Year. Meanwhile some of the others in the billet had seen me helping Jock with his letters and asked for my assistance. To compensate me for the time and effort and to avoid being overwhelmed, I decided to charge half a crown, (12.5p present day), per letter but still found my services much in demand. I was glad of the extra money since army pay was 13 shillings and 6 pence per week and most of it went on cleaning materials for kit and boots. Before my newfound wealth I had known the desperate feeling of having no money left at the end of a week.

One night in late November when I was feeling low I left the confines of the billet to take a walk around the barracks. It had been raining and an icy wind sharpened the air. Near the camp perimeter, which couldn't be crossed without a Pass, there was a large wooden hut with light spilling from its windows and the sound of music within. A man in a peaked cap and dark uniform stepped from the shadows and hailed me.

"Come inside and have something to eat and drink." I thanked him and explained that I had no money. Back came the reply which I have never forgotten. "God's love costs nothing. It's a free gift for everyone. You're welcome. Come inside!"

The reception within the hut was warm and cosy. There were tables and chairs spread around and an iron stove centre piece rendered the room snug and inviting. An older woman wearing an apron like my grandmother's handed me a hot mug of coffee and ushered me to a table where there were plates of sandwiches and small cakes. A wireless was playing light music and the atmosphere was homely and friendly, bringing tears to my eyes. The place was run by the Salvation Army but I was exposed to no sermonising or church doctrines. It was simply charity for the sake of humanity and the essence of goodness it embodied came straight from the heart. I was totally undone by the kindness extended to me and other lonely young men that cold evening. It was given without condition simply because it was needed. To this day I fondly remember that act of caring and support the Charity whenever I can.

It came to the day of the run. Tight booted and strapped in full uniform, wearing heavy kit bags on our backs, we set off in batches. The ground was hard with an early frost and the going at first was uphill. I made good headway running alongside Jock whose leviathan strides ate up the distance. We crossed tracks between straggling pine trees and over rocky inclines until at the three mile marker I began to falter and felt a stitch in my side. "You go on, Jock." I panted." I'm finished." "No way!" came the hearty reply. "We'll finish together."

Jock just about carried me over the finish line but even then I collapsed with exhaustion. All around there were groups of men retching from the effects of their efforts whilst Jock didn't even sit down but simply walked around smoking. I was tremendously grateful to him especially as two weeks later I triumphantly collected my ten day pass. I was bound for King's Cross station in London to travel on the eastern line to Newcastle-on-Tyne but Jock was sent to Bristol to take the western rail route to Glasgow. We shook hands and wished each other all the best as we departed on our different ways. I remember we waved each other away with warm smiles unaware that we would never see each other again.

I arrived in Newcastle at 3.00 a.m. on a very cold Christmas Eve morning. It was too early for any transport to be available and so I set off walking the three odd miles to my grandmother's house in Blaydon-on-Tyne. It was well after four when I reached the street where she lived, the sight of which brought back a rush of fond memories.

I could see a light in the bathroom window upstairs as my grandmother rose early to go to her cleaning jobs in the town. It was a heart- warming home coming filled with all the snugness and loving feelings of family. Uncle John was there too for the holiday and left his bed to join us for breakfast. I relaxed, it seemed, for the first time in months. I asked if I could spend my leave with them and they said they would be glad to have me. I handed over to my grandmother most of my army pay to help with the Christmas expenses for food. I'd brought gift wrapped presents for them which I added to the pile under the indoor Christmas tree all decked out in festive baubles and strands of glitter.

The news from my mother's house was much the same as usual except that my eldest sister, (half-sister), had passed the late entry for grammar school but had withdrawn because she wouldn't take showers with the other girls after games lessons. Once again I was faced with evidence of the ill effects of our repressive upbringing blighting our living. Later in the day I paid a short visit to see my mother and give her a present. She was shocked to see my shaven head and how much weight I'd lost. As I sat and drank a cup of tea in the lounge I heard my father laughing in the kitchen as he berated my mother for worrying about me. "The army will knock the ponce out of the boy. Do him the world of good." His voice sounded louder than usual, probably to make sure that I heard his comments. Nothing changes with him and his attitude to me, I thought.

As was customary in the family there were no presents for me but my mother mentioned that that I might like a dressing gown from the Co-op to take back with me. I told her not to bother as the army did not allow us to wear civilian clothes whilst in training. I left as soon as I could to escape the feelings of depression the place always aroused.

Later I walked to Axewell Park and spent some time meditating in the woods to refresh myself. On the way back to my grandmother's house I stopped for a while to watch a flock of lapwings, sometimes called green plovers, circling above an area of marsh in a field next to the cemetery. Their plaintive cries of 'Peewit, Peewit' echoing against the bleak backdrop of a wintry sky did much to restore my feelings of sang-froid towards my home and the army. The sight of their flight as they wheeled and banked in the air like miniature Tiger Moth aeroplanes, never failed to raise my spirits. Here again, barely a day back in my native haunts, I was feeling the healing power of Nature. It was good to be back home. I felt a warmth inside to be here and looked forward to the delights of my grandmother's cooking and her company and that of Uncle John over the Christmas.

All too soon it was time to leave. I felt revived by the homecoming and the uplifting loving company. Unable to find a seat on the crowded train going back I sat on my suitcase in the small corridor between the coaches and read from a book of sea stories, one of my Christmas presents. In my case I had packed a small spiced fruit cake and two pairs of knitted thick woollen socks, mementos of the homely warmth I had indulged in over the festive season. They would serve me well in the spartan conditions of the barracks to which I was returning.

The first news to greet me was that Jock had been killed in a fight on New Year's Eve. The Sergeant said that he'd heard that he had been murdered by one of the notorious Glaswegian gangs and that the police were investigating. The news devastated and saddened me. I felt that I had lost a good friend. There were several other vacant beds in my billet of men who had gone AWOL, (Absent Without Leave).

Without remit the pace of army training resumed its relentless tempo and I found myself posted to Willems Barracks on the outskirts of Aldershot to join a group undergoing clerk training interspersed with periods of parade ground drill and weapons instruction. The latter I really enjoyed and was pleased to gain first class level on the Lee Enfield Rifle and also the Sten Gun, a hand held semi-automatic machine gun made famous by WWII commandos. All recruits, as soldiers in training, were obliged to learn to fire a rifle and most men managed to accomplish this but there was one who began to cry and bubble when instructed to adopt the firing position. Lying prone facing the shooting butts he was told to aim his rifle at the target five hundred yards away and fire five rounds. But he simply freaked out. He just couldn't or wouldn't fire his weapon. The Sergeant in charge of weapons training tried all ways to get him to comply without success. Eventually the Sergeant ordered me to lie alongside this recruit and man handle him through the exercise of firing at the target whilst he stood astride behind us. Lying down beside him and adopting the firing position I took the man's right hand in mine and reluctantly forced him to hold the magazine of .303 cartridges and load them into his rifle. I told him as gently as I could that it was best to get it over with and that I was here to help him. Then I manipulated his hand to undo and pull back the bolt and ram it forward and lock it to insert a cartridge into his rifle. I lined his weapon to point at the target and pushed his fore-finger into the trigger guard. Next I wrapped my finger around his and pulled until it fired. I did this five times and then rendered the breech open to the safe position. During this process the man sobbed and blubbered in my face without speaking. When I'd finished the Sergeant complimented me and explained that every recruit had to have fired his rifle and have it written in his pass book. He, as the non commissioned officer in charge, (NCO), was not allowed to do it for him and he was much obliged to me for my help. The recruit was dismissed and ordered back to his billet. He never spoke a word during the whole experience and I did not see him ever again. I did wonder how he would cope with bayonet practice and the unarmed combat sessions.

In six weeks I had qualified on the typewriter, (40 words a minute) and Army Office procedures. I was then informed that I had been listed to take a War Office Selection Board Interview, (WOSBI), in the selection process for officer training. Whilst I was waiting I was assigned to the Company Sergeant Major's office as his company clerk. Sergeant Major Art Rumbold was a distinguished veteran of World War II. I later learned that he was an orphan and had enlisted as a boy soldier. He had served with distinction in a front line infantry unit during the War. He was festooned with war service medals and ribbons and had earned numerous citations for outstanding bravery under fire. But now as he eked out his time before retirement he had developed a cantankerous demeanour to all and sundry but especially towards recruits. At my first meeting with him I was scorched with the blasphemy of his profane language so much so that I decided to ask the Company Commander for a different job. When he stopped to draw breath I respectfully told him so and turned to leave. All at once he changed, barked at me to sit down and offered me a drink from his private hoard of single malt scotch whiskey which he kept in a cupboard labelled 'Company Orders. "There now" he said as I took the proffered drink "Let's have no more talk of going to the 'shit for brains' CO. You can be on a cushy number here 'cos all you have to do is keep me right on all these new-fangled regulations and I'll see you all right with passes and things. As he proceeded to again pour whiskey in my glass I realised that he was desperate for help and doubtless I was his last hope since others before me had probably refused to work for him. Just how desperate for help he was quickly became clear when I found out that he was all but illiterate and an alcoholic to boot. When he saw that I was prepared to stay he told me that we needed to sort out Company Orders for the weekend, today being Friday. He mentioned a couple of items that had to go in them and then handed me a file containing past orders and said that I should have them typed and ready for his signature by five o'clock or 1700 hours army time. Since it was now the middle of the afternoon I was thrown into a state of near panic especially when he made to leave and said that he wouldn't be back.

"What about your signature?" I asked.

"Oh that's alright just you sign them and put them on the notice board and lock up the office." At this comment he tossed me a large bunch of keys and bade me goodbye.

"I'll be in the Sergeant's Mess if anybody wants me."

Over the following weeks my daily state of panic gradually subsided as I became more familiar with the simple procedures of the office routine. Anything that required writing or typing and signing was my job whilst my boss Sergeant Major Rumbold regaled me as I worked with his wartime exploits. After he had consumed his daily bottle of whiskey he liked to take a nap and woe betide anyone who disturbed him. I began to relax and enjoy the freedom which the position of company clerk afforded until one morning, around seven thirty, as I made my way to the office, I was stopped by a Staff Sergeant who ordered me to dress in full kit and report to the Guard House for guard duties. As a Private I had no option but to obey and so I left the keys with the CO's orderly and dressed in my best uniform in preparation for inspection and guard duties. When Sergeant Major Rumbold discovered what had happened the ensuing pandemonium must have seemed as if World War III had broken out and even the CO retreated to the Officers' Mess for sanctuary. After my twenty four hour stint of guarding the Company I was tired and in need of sleep but the Sergant Major was waiting for me as I left the Guard House. "Why didn't you refuse the order and say that you worked for me!" And so he harangued me for over an hour because I hadn't been there to run his office. Eventually I summoned up the courage to tell him that as a Private and a recruit at that I had no rights when ordered to do something by a high ranking NCO. He exploded with temper when I told him this and yelling and swearing enough to turn the air blue he charged out of the office. Peace at last, I thought as I set to do my clerical duties. However he reappeared two hours later smirking from ear to ear. "You're promoted to Sergeant, temporary while you work for me." I was flabbergasted. "But does the CO know?"

I asked tentatively. "Who do you think ordered it?" He thundered back at me." Now go and get those flashes on your arms before somebody else grabs you for duties. You work for me and only me will have the say what your duties are." When I thought about it I suppose it was not unusual to have an NCO in charge of an office, the Pay Corps always had a Sergeant in charge of procedures. Anyway it was not my doing but it was a stroke of fortune and I determined to enjoy it as long as it lasted. My promotion was listed on Company orders and I found that I was now entitled to a room of my own at the end of a billet. Also I was given a pay rise which eased my life no end.

I hurried away to the Taylor's Shop to change my uniform. I must admit that I was slightly worried by this development especially in view of what the reactions of other NCOs would be, but I needn't have bothered because no one dared say a word against Sergeant Major Rumbold. From the next day on, Sergeant O'Connor was established as the Company Clerk. I soon grew accustomed to the authority I now had on the whim of a tyrant whom I suspected was mentally unbalanced with psychotic tendencies. But he treated me well as long as I coped with all the demands. In this respect it was I who wrote out Company Orders and it was I who signed every letter, order and pass in the Sergeant Major's name. No one checked my work since my boss spent the day in a state of euphoric alcoholic fantasy from whence, if disturbed, his fury knew no bounds. One day a well- meaning young officer insisted on seeing the Sergeant Major despite my cautions. He wanted to post an item on Company Orders inviting volunteers to join a Country Dance Group. When the young officer's request finally penetrated the Sergeant Major's drunken haze there was an explosion little short of nuclear. I hastened to intervene and shepherded the emotionally stricken officer safely back outside before he suffered a physical assault. I don't think the young man had ever heard such a volume of expletives in all his life. Before he left I told him that I'd insert his item in the Company Orders and he passed me a slip of paper with the details. Looking decidedly dazed he thanked me and made a quick exit.

Sometimes I took an hour off when things were quiet in the office. I always told the Sergeant Major that I was taking a short break and would be back directly. As long as he was told he didn't mind but if he'd found me gone without his knowledge he would panic and pandemonium would ensue.

On my breaks I sought out rural settings and fortunately there was a patch of forest surrounded by fields and rough gorseland nearby. It was sometimes used for training purposes involving stealth activities such as sniper training and commando tactics. For me it was a relief to wander freely among the trees and listen to the bird song, it was a blissful change from poring over army regulations and memoranda from HQ. There were rare period of delight when the woods fell silent and nothing stirred except a breeze rustling the leaves in soothing murmurs. Then it seemed as if time had hushed the world to rest and every living thing was in tranquil slumber. While the earth and the entire cosmos hardly seemed to move, I stood motionless in the cool of the shade and allowed the stillness to saturate my senses with contentment.

I recall one day I was leaning on a fence with my back to the woods when unexpectedly a pony sought me out. She snorted and whickered as she trotted over the field to greet me. She had a bright glow about her that was almost unreal, just as if she'd trotted out of a fairy tale. Glossy fawn coloured hair covered her back and flanks and she had a long blonde mane. Gentle brown eyes expressed her need for solace, having been left alone. Horses are herd animals and prefer not to be solitary. She was lonely but certainly belonged to someone because she'd was wearing a new leather head band. I stroked her and told her that I was lonely too, lonesome for my wild animal friends who were far away from me. We got along just fine sharing good company as we spent an hour together watching a snowy owl roving the long grasses hunting rodents. The pony, I thought, probably belonged to some officer's daughter and was kept as a token pet.

Reluctantly I left her and returned to find the Sergeant Major standing just outside the office haranguing two recruits about the length of their hair. He immediately collared me and insisted that I put an item in Company

Orders stressing the need for recruits to have short haircuts. I was beginning to grow weary of my formidable mentor but I did enjoy my good fortune in having sergeant's pay even though I had a premonition it wouldn't last much longer.

Matters came to a head sooner than I expected. Thursday morning was my 'Catch Up' day when items I had put aside were given full attention. I also used the time for filing since it was easy to be overwhelmed by the amount of paperwork the army generated. Sergeant Major Rumbold appeared briefly staying only sufficient time to have two large slugs of whiskey from the bottle in his desk drawer. We didn't exchange any words as he could see I was busy but there was something about his demeanour which alerted me and, in the midst of my work, I recall thinking he's after causing trouble over something or other. I was not wrong. There came the sound of pounding of feet and amongst the pounding came the sounds of bellowing and yelling. I recognised his voice at once. He was in the process of arousing new recruits from their beds in billets on the third floor of a building to parade on the square below. Some of them having reached ground level had collapsed whilst many of the others were obviously suffering dizzy spells as they tried to obey the shouted commands. I didn't believe that he knew what he was doing.

The recruits in question were in distress after having mandatory injections the previous day which afforded them, by medical authority, forty eight hours respite to recuperate

Wild Adventures in Time and Place

from the effects. Sergeant Rumbold had discovered these men in bed during his drunken wanderings and had become enraged. But these men were in no fit state to do any square bashing. I ran up to the Sergeant Major and tried to tell him about the men's condition but he refused to listen to me and continued to bark out drill commands and thrash the ground with his long stick. My only recourse was to phone the Medical Officer, (MO), and explain what was happening. Minutes later I was relieved to see from my office window the MO and the Duty Officer arriving in haste. There followed a confrontation of sorts with the result that the Sergeant Major left the scene just as a group of medical orderlies arrived to shepherd the sick recruits back to their beds.

Sergeant Major Rumbold did not re-appear until the following morning and it was the first time I had seen him sober. He explained to me that the CO had demanded that he retire with immediate effect. So he had come to thank me and to say goodbye. I wished him all the very best and we shook hands. He departed immediately and I wondered what would happen to him. The Army was his life so where could he go. Meanwhile I carried on with my clerking duties awaiting outcomes. I did not have long to wait as a new man, Sergeant Major Jobson, was appointed to take charge of the office and I was asked to stay on until my posting arrived. I liked him and we worked together well as I showed him what I knew of the routines. I felt a weight lifted off my shoulders as he took overall responsibility for what went into Company Orders and dealt with everything requiring a signature.

A pleasant distraction for me at this time was the posting of a detachment of cavalry to part of the battalion complex. I lost no time in introducing myself to the NCOs in charge and was privileged to be allowed to visit the stables and meet the horses. The fact that I wore sergeant stripes no doubted facilitated my acceptance amongst their company. I have always loved horses and these were exceptional animals, trained and groomed to perfection. The Cavalry Company had been sent to Aldershot in preparation for a visit by Her Majesty Queen Elizabeth in June to celebrate her official birthday and so there was much drilling and coordinated parading which I took great pleasure in watching whenever I could. The Sergeant Major in charge of the unit could not but help notice my interest and invited me to join him over a drink. The upshot was that I was invited to ride one of the horses during the evening when the cavalry men were bulling their equipment or relaxing. Sergeant Major Driscoll arranged to meet me in front of the huge shed which had been converted into an indoor riding arena. Wearing fatigues and soft shoes I entered the training arena at the appointed time and was greeted by the Sergeant Major standing by a black horse of at least seventeen hands in height. But what surprised me most was that the horse had no saddle. "You can ride bareback can you?" It sounded more like a statement of fact rather than a question.

"Er... No, I never tried" I said nervously beginning to feel apprehensive.

"Well, it's high time you did. If you can't ride bareback you haven't learned to ride. Now come and get up here." And with that he grabbed me by the backside and flung me astride the Black which stood rock still never flinching. Feeling decidedly insecure without a saddle and stirrups, I tentatively held the reins and kneed the horse to move. At once, from a standing start, the Black moved into a rocking cantor and I slid all the length off its back to hit the ground with a thud. "What on earth are you trying to do?"

"Not fall off" I said, rubbing my backside ruefully. "I can see we have some learning to do. For one thing you need to master the technique of relaxing when you fall off. Now stand and hold your horse and take heed to what I say." I rapidly became aware that the mode of the evening had changed from an entertaining interlude to hard work. He began his instruction born of long practice instructing recruits to the cavalry.

"First of all you should wrap your legs around the horse's body as if your life depended on it. Cling like glue with your knees and thighs so that nothing short of a bomb can unseat you. Possess your horse so that whatever the horse does, wherever it might move, you go with it. Now get up there Mister and let's see some horse riding!"

For the next hour I mounted and re-mounted the Big Black called Demetrius. I clung with desperation to his back as he fast trotted around the indoor ring. Just when I managed to survive a circuit bareback the Sergeant Major would ride up alongside me and, with a wild thrust of his arm, knock me off the horse. By the end of the first week of our evening sessions, I was black and blue and purple all over. After which he would haul me away, despite my protestations, for a heavy bout of drinking in the Sergeants' Mess. After two and a half weeks of such 'torture' I could more or less perform competently riding bareback. I learned to physically withstand his attempts to unseat me by gripping the horse with my legs and thighs as if my life depended on it. Eventually there came an evening session when I began to indulge in the joy of riding and feeling at one with the horse in a way I had never known despite my previous riding experience. Over a drink on the last night of our association, since his detachment was due to pull out the following day, I thanked him for his instruction.

"Well I had nothing better to do and you needed to learn proper riding. You know, the Red Indian Tribes in the U.S.A. (now called Native Americans), especially the Commanches, rode bareback into battle, firing their arrows and sometimes rifles from the back of a horse. Military Commanders fighting against them at the time, early to middle of the nineteenth century, rated them amongst the best cavalry in the world. Once you've learned to ride bareback then riding with a saddle and stirrups is child's play.

I took time off the next day to watch their departure, long horse transporters and lorries filled with equipment and men, it was like watching a circus on the move. The Queen's Birthday parade had gone off without a hitch and now they were all de- camping back to their stable barracks in London. I would miss the companionship and other talents of Sergeant Major Driscoll to whom I owed a great deal.

∽

The next morning as I prepared my work Sergeant Major Jobson came into my office wearing a solemn expression. "I've just heard" he said gravely "That Sergeant Major Rumbold committed suicide."

"How?" I asked, suspecting that my worst fears had been realized. He took the train down to Eastbourne and a taxi to Beachy Head. He had been drinking in the local pub and then he walked to the cliffs and jumped off. Apparently he was wearing full dress uniform with all his medals."

For a while I sat stunned, unsure of what to say. At last I found some words: "He was very proud of his country." Sergeant Major Jobson nodded "So I believe."It would suit him to die by the White Cliffs. For him they would signify the England he had fought to preserve." I continued, imagining how he would be thinking in those final moments.

"I expect you're right" the Sergeant Major said and walked back into his office. Quite suddenly I felt an impulse to turn and look outside my window, there perched on the top of the fire hydrant, a Magpie stared in at me. We gazed at each other for a while and then the bird flew off. For the rest of the afternoon I couldn't help thinking of Sergeant Major Art Rumbold. Perhaps the Magpie had brought me a message. Who can tell? Anyway I never saw the bird again.

Two weeks later my posting came through for the Officer Selection Board which was to be held over three days at Buller Barracks. I was to leave in two days, time enough for me to settle everything in the office. I would, of course, have to revert to the rank of Private. I was glad to be moving on and I relished the opportunity to leave the traumas of working for the late Sergeant Major Rumbold behind me. The posting heralded a new beginning in my Army career which is another story entirely but not for the telling here.

The day I was demobbed was a fine sunny day in June 1955. I was given leave to cover the last few weeks of my time in the Army and as I left the War Office Building, where I'd spent the last eight months, the feelings of relief at being a free man again were tantamount to being reborn. Dressed in civilian clothes I headed cheerfully by London Tube for the train at King's Cross. Seated in the luxury of a First Class carriage drinking from a plastic mug of British Rail coffee I was as content as a man could be. Suddenly my calm demeanour was shattered by what I saw from my window seat. Two burly military policemen were charging up the platform staring hawkishly into each compartment of the stationary train. All at once my mind raced back to the office in Whitehall where I'd served the Machiavellian and manic Major Rospoi-Lesmatin in command of Army Field Intelligence. It would be just like him to have me brought forcibly back on a whim of his to attend to an item I'd unwittingly left undone. My heart froze as the two officers reached my window and glared in at me. Then the moment passed without incident and seconds later I saw them dragging away a young man along the platform. I sat back in the cushioned seat and unwound just as the train began slowly to move out of the station. It was over I told myself and I really was free. Now I could look forward to my university studies and the prospects of a career and a new life.

The Engagement

A faded greetings card found among the detritus of my late mother's worldly goods read:

"Congratulations on your engagement and all good wishes for your future happiness." The signature was indecipherable.

That was all. But then I had heard versions of the engagement many times from my mother and grandmother. It all stemmed from a meeting between the two families on a particular Saturday at one o'clock in February 1932. That was all that had been agreed.

The temperature outside was freezing, with an icy wintry chill in the air, as the two families gathered in the Church hall. Several of them trembled with the cold despite their winter clothing as the coke stove struggled vainly to spread some warmth. Out of doors the brutal North Wind was already blowing flurries of snow as it rattled the draughty windows of the hall and caused the timbers of the roof to creak and groan.

A man, dressed in an old overcoat, worn brown tweed suit, white shirt and a frayed green tie stood and stared cold eyed at the two groups sitting before him. He held himself tensely erect radiating a dignity commensurate with his advanced age that was in no way limited by his frail build.

He began to speak and in speaking his voice betrayed the angst he felt as he conveyed his words in a soft spoken Southern Irish brogue.

"My name is Gerard O'Sullivan and I am here in the company of some of my grown children who are, together with my wife Mary and the children who could not be here, my only family. We are meeting here rather than in our home as befits the contentious nature of the issues here to be addressed."

Here he paused to turn and gesture to the group sitting directly behind him as if to ensure their support before turning to face the smaller party in front of him.

"I have come to meet here with the family of Rita Watson. My son, Bernard, has asked my permission to marry the young lady called Rita whom, I am told, is the only daughter in your family."

His eyes singled out an attractive young brunette who sat clutching the lapels of her coat tightly to her breast not just because of the cold. She sat close to her mother and her mother's brother as they alone were confronted by the old man and his family sitting opposite.

O'Sullivan coughed a chesty cough which racked his sparse frame and momentarily prevented him from speaking. The cough was a legacy from years of working at the local coke ovens.

"There is however, a problem which needs to be resolved before we can proceed further in this matter irrespective of the feelings of the two young people involved since this is a matter requiring the compliance and wider sanction of family."

He coughed again before breathlessly continuing, letting his eyes rove the room as if to challenge any possible dissent.

"The young woman my son has chosen is not of our religious faith and therefore it is not possible for us to countenance a union which is contrary to our deeply held beliefs and spiritual commitment."

At this point two women in his family group took out rosary beads and sliding the beads between trembling fingers began to silently mouth a fervent litany with eyes half closed in concentration.

"Unless she is prepared to convert to Roman Catholicism there can be no marriage. That is my resolve and final word on which there is no possibility of negotiation."

In the silence that followed the old man took his seat beside his sons on the front row bench and looked across expectantly at the young woman's family.

After some furtive whispering amongst the small group, the girl's Uncle, John Watson, rose and addressed the family sitting opposite in a well spoken, gentle but authoritative voice.

"Rita, my niece, who is already a baptised Christian, is willing to convert to your religion even though it is against my advice and the wishes of her mother. We will, nonetheless, support her in the proposed relationship with your son. I am

Wild Adventures in Time and Place

sure the arrangements for this can be amicably conducted from here on. We would have much preferred to meet with you in our home where it would at least have been more comfortable."

Since no reply was forthcoming and with the essentials for the present having been made clear, the girl and her mother stood and the Uncle, by way of tactfully drawing the meeting to a close, finally said:

"Let us all now go home in peace and get warm."

The two groups left without exchanging any parting greetings. The young couple, who were the focus of the assembly, glanced briefly at each other from opposite ends of the room without speaking. Outside the air was glacial and even the crows, black sentinels roosting high in the trees above the churchyard, appeared committed to suffer the cruel chill. For the departing people below them the prospects appeared to be equally bleak.

The engagement ritual between the families was over. It could not be called a party as such nor could it be called an engagement proper but perhaps it heralded the pledge of an engagement. It was evident that much had yet to pass from what had been stated on that wintry Saturday afternoon.

Once she was out of what had been for her the stifling formality of the exchanges in the hall, Rita turned to her mother and began to talk breezily as if a clamp had been lifted from her tongue.

"Gosh, it was freezing in there in more ways than one.
"What did you make of it, mother?"

Elizabeth Watson normally wore a happy facial expression but now she looked pained and drawn.

"I can't see you having much chance of happiness with that family. They don't seem a bit like us. They are foreigners, Rita. They don't appreciate how we are and that old man will want to dominate you like he obviously governs his family."

The tone of resignation in her voice as she said this was palpable. Before responding to her mother's words Rita turned to her Uncle.

"What did you think, Uncle?"

John Watson took his time in making a reply because he didn't want to dash the high hopes held by his beloved niece. A kindly man, the air of hostility seeping through from the other family into the atmosphere of the meeting had disturbed him. But now, for Rita's sake, he attempted to strike a more positive note than he in fact felt.

"I believe that if you put your heart and soul into the relationship, not only with your young man but with his family, it could work. But are you prepared for such an all out commitment to a marriage, which may itself be difficult enough, but also to a new, unfamiliar religion?"

Wild Adventures in Time and Place

The words from her mother and uncle caused an uneasiness within her to surface and shadowy doubts began to dampen her hitherto flushed romantic expectations. Not wishing to pursue this depressing line of thought any further she abruptly, girl like, changed the subject completely without any attempt at making an answer. Instead she responded with a radiant eyed smile for them both as if she hadn't a care in the world.

"Let's call in at Brennan's and buy some fish and chips for our supper."

In contrast to the slightly more sanguine viewpoint of the Watsons, the mood in the O'Sullivans' family group was funereal. Kathleen, the eldest daughter and one of the women who had pulled out their rosary beads during the meeting, was the first to break the silence as they headed homewards up the hill, walking slowly to accommodate their father's breathless plodding.

"Dad, why don't you send our Bernard over to Ireland for a while so he can get to know some of the old country's beautiful colleens?"

She attempted to make the suggestion light hearted but she meant it seriously enough all the same.

Her father gave her an affectionate but condescending smile.

"I know what you're trying to say, Katie, but Ireland has nothing to offer us anymore and besides young Bernard has only just started his joinery apprenticeship at the Co-op. No we'll just have to pray that this will all work out for the best, God willing."

Kate was tearful as the hopelessness of his reply struck home. One of the few members of the family who'd been born in Ireland before they emigrated, she was fiercely proud of her roots.

"Well, she'll never be accepted into our family if I know my mother!"

Her father sighed resignedly

"Yes, you're right Kate in thinking how your mother will react to this. Mary will be after dealing with this in her own sweet way but she'll never willingly hand over one of her sons to a non catholic girl; and an English one at that."

It had all started in the months before Christmas when groups of adolescents gathered of an evening within Blaydon Town Square to look each other over and indulge in fanciful posturing and flirting. One night when the exchanges were in full swing a vivacious looking girl approached a dark haired lad sitting astride his bicycle and brazenly blew out the candle in his cycle lamp. Taken aback at her audacity but flattered at the contact he demanded her name.

"I'm called Rita; what's your name?"

"Bernard but people call me Brian."

Then abruptly before he lost his nerve

"Will you go out with me?"

"Well, the nerve of you!"

After a lengthy pause during which she scrutinized him intently "I might think about it."

From that time onwards whenever the young people met, especially at weekends, Rita and Brian began to seek out each other's company as if that first brief encounter had sown a seed of mutual attraction. At first it seemed to happen by accident rather than design but later it was to assume a more serious aspect. Eventually they would break away from contact with the group, as they jointly sought the comfort of each other's company during walks together by the River Tyne.

It was some time before they worked up the nerve to hold hands and then only when they were strictly alone. One dark night they exchanged a tentative kiss which was far from passionate but started them to light heartedly discuss romantic plans for the future which at this stage were fancifully non-committal. Visits to the cinema together followed but still their friendship was casual and interspersed with apparent cooling off periods when they did not see each other for days. One evening, after due consideration but seemingly on impulse, she invited him to come for tea with her family at the weekend.

She had deliberately chosen Sunday for his visit because she knew that her mother always called on friends during the evening and her uncle would be helping out at the local

Anglican Church Services. She had invited him to come at 4.30 p.m. which only gave an hour before it was time for everyone to go their different ways. By this strategy she managed both to 'break the ice' with her family about her boy friend and at the same time avoid undue embarrassment on his part. The 'Tea party' went off well with all concerned on their best behaviour and Rita was delighted to see that Brian did his best to make a good impression. From that occasion on their relationship deepened and they became a regular couple contemplating engagement with a view to eventual marriage. At this stage there was no involvement with his family although the prospect of breaking the news of the courtship to his parents loomed large on his mind. Eventually his anxiety would allow no further delay and as the family sat down to dinner one evening he nervously blurted out his 'secret.' A stunned silence followed the disclosure punctuated by gasps of incomprehension. With a wail of anguish his mother fled the table clutching the lower flap of her apron to her face. All eyes now focused on the father who sat stiffly as if immobilized by the revelation. Carefully placing his knife and fork on the table and, wiping his lips with a handkerchief, Gerard O'Sullivan stared hard at his second youngest son. When he spoke it was in the tradition of an Irish patriarch and ruler of his family.

"There'll be no more talk of this until later when I will find the truth of the matter and decide what has to be done, that is when I have had time to talk with your mother. This is a family concern. You have seen how you have upset her and we'll have to see what will and will not be allowed. After all we are a Catholic family and live according to the will and by the grace of God, we are not given to heathen ways."

After the silence following the mother's abrupt departure and the speech from their father, a sudden babble of chatter broke out around the table as if to dispel the tension and convey the pretence that all was well but underneath a seething undercurrent of alarm was surfacing in the minds of all those present.

There was no sign of their mother for the rest of the meal. The table was cleared and the dishes washed without her usual commanding presence. Sighing heavily Gerard O'Sullivan laboriously mounted the stairs to their bedroom and found his wife kneeling before a statue of the Virgin, tears streaming down her cheeks. He settled on the bare wooden chair by their bed and waited for her to acknowledge his presence. After a while she rose and without turning or looking at him said:

"You'll be going to our priest and you'll be asking for his advice. Take this ten shilling note from my housekeeping, which I can ill afford, but which will pay for a Mass to be said for God's help. You will be seeing our Bernard and finding out how far this thing has gone. I will not have any peace until it has all been done."

She then lay down fully clothed on the bed and began to sob into the bed sheet which she held to her face. Her feelings were in ferment at the changes taking place within her family. The myth of being able to transpose their Irish village culture to their newly adopted country was slowly being dismantled. Now the oldest boys, especially Tony and Chris, spent most evenings playing snooker and billiards whilst smoking and drinking beer in the Catholic League room next to the Church, something that would never have been allowed back home. She felt that she was losing her own identity and power befitting an Irish mother with twelve children.

"Oh Lord, save us before we abandon the Faith of our fathers" she wailed into the gathering gloom of the room.

There would be no rest in the house for their parents that night. Aware of this the family moved about quietly as if walking on eggshells and each person held their tongue or spoke only in whispers until they could take their leave.

Meanwhile their father sat alone in the tiny box room he used as his private sanctuary. With his wife's words coursing through his mind he pondered what to do. Bernard had already left the house so it would be late before he could be confronted and as for consulting the priest that would have to wait for another day since he had yet to ascertain the facts.

When Bernard, who now always called himself Brian, met with Rita that evening she bombarded him with questions:

"Did you break the news to your family?" and at the sight of his sombre nod

"What did they say, tell me, tell me quickly?". "I told them at dinner. They were shocked. My mother left the table in tears. My father was really angry and reminded me that we were not heathens. It was awful and I left as quickly as I could but no doubt there'll be an inquisition when I get back."

They tried to put the matter on hold for the moment but the worry about what the outcome would be dampened their spirits and they parted for the night earlier than usual. When Brian returned home his father, as he had feared, was waiting for him.

"Tell me, Bernard, exactly what is going on between you and this girl?"

"We've been friends for some time and we love each other and want to get married and set up home."

It poured out of him and his father was taken aback by the strength of will in his words.

"But what of her family?"

"I have met with her mother and her Uncle and they appear to have accepted us as the courting couple we are."

At this his father turned red in the face and in a flash of anger cried out:

"This has gone far enough without our family having any say at all!"

Then as he regained his composure he spoke very deliberately to his son whom he could see had adopted a defiant stance.

"Now there will have to be a meeting between the families and an understanding reached before we go any further; that is all I have to say at the moment. I will instruct Anthony and Dan to arrange this meeting somewhere but not here. You must help with the arrangements and get the agreement of this girl's family to meet with us. Is that clearly understood?"

Satisfied with his father's decision Brian simply nodded and quickly left the room for bed, relieved at last that things were moving forwards.

Following the formal meeting of the two families Gerard O'Sullivan took it upon himself, as prompted by his wife, to visit St. Joseph's Roman Catholic Church ostensibly to arrange instruction for Rita Watson to facilitate her conversion to the Catholic Faith. Only that wasn't his only intention. After the evening service he knocked on the door of the vestry whilst Father Patrick O'Brien, a mature man in his mid fifties, was putting away his vestments. The priest welcomed him as someone among his parishioners whom he knew very well. Scrutinising the old man's facial expression he gathered this to be a serious call on his services and motioned him to one of two wooden armchairs, the second of which he sat in himself. He smiled across at the man before him.

"What can I help you with Gerard?" he intoned encouragingly. Old man O'Sullivan explained the situation with regard to his son's intended betrothal to a non catholic girl but then added something which caused the priest's face to darken and made him stand up and angrily confront his parishioner. In spite of religious protocol O'Sullivan had asked:

"Father my wife and I, for our family's sake, would be forever obliged if you could find a way to dissuade this young lady from joining our Church and therefore of entertaining ideas of marrying our son."

There it was said and done. O'Sullivan let out a deep sigh at the effort it had taken to vent his words and leaned back in his chair as he waited for the priest's response.

Father O'Brien was normally a temperate man but now he turned angrily on O'Sullivan and the wrath of God fuelled the words that exploded from him. Leaving his seat he stood and confronted his parishioner with all the verbal force he could muster.

"How dare you?" he roared. "How dare you ask a priest of God to do blasphemous work in the cause of Satan? You are a sinful man O'Sullivan and if you pursue what you have just now intimated to me I shall excommunicate the lot of you and Jesus Christ himself will visit a curse on your family for all eternity."

Abashed and mortified by the priest's words Gerard O'Sullivan fell to his knees and sobbed a plea for forgiveness. Through his tears he mouthed the excuses of Irish family honour which had driven him at his wife's request to make such an ill advised demand. His temper abating somewhat the priest placed a hand on the old man's head and implored him to be calm.

"You're a troubled soul right enough O'Sullivan. Now take yourself home and the mercy of Christ be upon you and your family. We'll hear no more of this. I will expect that you arrange for your son and this young lady to call upon me sooner rather than later and we will put this matter in hand. I will not refuse another soul in need of Our Blessed Lord's redemption. Now be off with you and in your heart you can be after thanking God for all He's done for you and your family."

It was a chastened but strangely relieved man who returned home that evening. After praying in front of the statue of the Christ in his room he managed to sum up enough courage to go to his wife and relate to her the words of Father O'Brien. She was in their bedroom lying awake on the bed. It was no use. She would not be comforted and continued to blubber and moan into her pillow. On the morn she would rise and go about her business as a dutiful wife and mother but for now she would lament the lost dream of her Celtic Catholic heritage.

In a short time his father arranged for Bernard and the Girl to visit Father O'Brien and soon Rita was launched into the instruction which would result in her conversion to Catholicism. This proved to be an enlightening and happy time for her except that a shadow was cast over her relationship with Brian since she was never made welcome in his home. His mother would not entertain the idea of seeing let alone speaking to her. When the couple met of an evening, whilst Rita was often upbeat and cheerful Brian, on the other hand, appeared increasingly morose and anxious. The reason was that he was receiving the "Treatment," which meant that within his family he was subjected to an emotional distancing by his mother and sisters. When he eventually confided in Rita she said they were being 'Cold Shouldered.' Not only that but the 'Bitchiness' that Brian had to endure was often verbal amounting to insulting comments about Rita who was variously referred to as 'An English Slut' and all the more hurtfully as a 'Daughter of the Devil.' All of this depressed the young couple and the strain upon their relationship led to a kind of siege mentality. Their love for each other assumed threatening aspects and they became increasingly down hearted. They tottered on the verge of despair,

Brian's brothers were disturbed by these developments. Tony, the eldest, and Dan, the youngest, in particular spoke harshly to their sisters about their bitchy attitudes but to no avail. Now Rita and Brian began to suffer the torment of indecision. Young love, especially first love, is a powerful emotional force which may not be thwarted but can turn inwards and become destructive. As time went by there was no let up in the negative vibes targeting their relationship. Indeed one day, Brian's sister Katie made a visit to the corner shop where Rita worked and, in a shameful onslaught, accused her of every nefarious intention against her brother and his family. Word got around and people began to gossip. News of this came to the ears of Rita's mother and Uncle and they responded angrily and caused Rita more upset. The couple became increasingly depressed and found little comfort in their time together. There were some vexed exchanges leading to shouting rows. Somehow their love for one another survived but it was no longer uplifting. Since there seemed little prospect of a beginning to what they desired, in mutual despair thoughts turned to an ending. They were both at their wit's end with worry. They considered parting but the very thought of terminating their relationship was abhorrent to them. Their feelings began to take another turn. Eventually they decided to end it all together. It was not a decision lightly reached but it was the only one they felt was open to them. They may not have been aware of it but they were afflicted with the same dilemma that other love torn lovers had suffered down the ages.

They met in church and made a pact with God. If they could not be together in this life then they would be united in love in the next. That is how their feelings disposed them. They each wrote letters of explanation to leave behind for the families to find. On a dry warm Friday night in June

Wild Adventures in Time and Place

they crossed the open fields and headed directly for their favourite spot by the Scotswood Bridge on the River Tyne.

Around midnight, by chance, Tony left his bed to use the backyard toilet. On return he noticed the note prominently displayed on the mantelpiece above the coal fire. It was addressed to his parents in a wavering hand which he recognised as belonging to his brother Bernard. All at once he became disturbed and had a sudden premonition. Snatching the letter and tearing it open he read the tear stained contents with mounting alarm. Rousing Chris and Dan, who shared his bedroom, he hurriedly questioned them. Shocked at being awakened it was Dan who sleepily recalled that his brother and Rita liked to meet by the Tyne Bridge at Scotswood. Tony, a born leader, now took charge.

"Get dressed Quick. It might already be too late!"

The three of them hurtled down the quiet terraced streets, the clatter of their boots on stony pavements arousing many a sleeping family from their rest. The brothers were young and fit and made short work of the distance to their objective but the desperate question in all of their minds was 'Would they be in time?' They mouthed fervent prayers to the Almighty as they breathlessly raced along.

By the Bridge the moonlight brightened the swirling waters of the River as the high tide reached its zenith. The couple desperately clutched each other, clasping tightly in a final loving embrace. As agreed it was Rita who went first. Stifling a sob she waded bare footed but fully clothed into the cold waters. Bernard followed striking out with his arms as if to swim across to the other side. They uttered no last words.

Tony saw them first, picking out two dark heads above the streaming currents. He yelled a warning to his brothers and then flung himself forward in a mad rugby dash. Diving headlong into the river he clutched Bernard just as he was about to sink again and out the corner of his eye he saw that Dan and Chris were lifting an unconscious Rita clear of the waves. Everyone was soaked to the skin but since the night was comparatively warm they suffered little from their ducking. A two man Bridge Patrol, alerted by their shouts, brought blankets and later some hot sweet tea. These patrol men were well used to saving potential suicides since the Bridge provided an exit opportunity for many poor souls who'd lost all hope.

"The young lady seems to be coming around alright" one of them called out as Rita stirred and coughed up some river water. The brothers were ecstatically triumphant that their rescue had been a success but it was Tony who voiced what the others felt. He swore softly before adamantly exclaiming

"This has gone far enough. It will be sorted out by me if nobody else!"

The other brothers nodded in agreement.

As soon as Brian got his breath back and could focus on what had happened he asked plaintively

"How did you know?"

Tony, momentarily pre-occupied with draining his boots and removing his wet socks, looked across at the pathetic sight of his younger brother drenched to the skin and just recently clutched from the jaws of death.

"I read your note. Oh, don't worry no one else has seen it. It's here in my pocket."

"Why did you do it?" Brian asked naively, staring at all three of them. Again it was Tony who answered.

"Listen to me, knothead! We're brothers and we are all in it together. Besides we had a fancy, although I can't think why, that we didn't want to lose you. Now I know that you've been having a hard time of it, you and your girl" and he looked across at Rita who was struggling to straighten her hair. "Well that is over. We," and here he glanced across to include Dan and Chris "We are going to sort it out and make an end to all the farce."

Brian hung his head shamefacedly and then reached out and hugged each of his brothers in turn.

Once Brian and Rita could walk the Bridge patrol urged them to be on their way in case the police appeared since attempting suicide was a criminal offence.

And with that five wet figures turned up at Rita's home. It was twenty minutes past three in the morning. The sky was already beginning to brighten as they were received by Rita's rudely awakened and much surprised mother. The letter above the fireplace was seized before her mother could see it and all was explained away as an accidental happening. As Rita blubbered in her mother's arms, the four brothers clasped hands and, though not a word was said, they were united in their resolve to reconcile their parents with Brian's hopes for a future with Rita. The coal fire was poked into blazing life and the brothers, blankets round their shoulders, sat in damp underwear as their outer clothing was hung up to dry. Rita, still tearful, joined them wrapped in her Uncle's dressing gown which was too big for her and emphasised her slight build and air of feminine vulnerability. Meeting the inquiring stares of the brothers she managed a rueful smile and they beamed back at her and soon everybody was smiling. A pan of left-over homemade broth was soon re-heated by her mother and served to the hungry company in an atmosphere of convivial relief. Elizabeth Watson looked over at the group of young people warming themselves at her fireside and realised that there was more to this incident than her daughter was telling her. But then it would all come out in due course as everything tended to do. For the moment she was content to ease whatever distress had brought them to her door with a warm unquestioning welcome.

Eight weeks later there was another meeting of the two families, this time in the parlour of the O'Sullivan house. Tony took the floor.

"We are here today to celebrate the engagement of my brother Bernard, who now calls himself Brian, to the lovely Rita. May God's blessing be upon them and all who are come here to wish them well."

There was a quick round of applause from those gathered which included the priest, Father O'Brien, the brothers and sisters O'Sullivan and even their father who sat in a corner and said nothing. His wife was upstairs feigning sickness but sent her blessing. There were plates of corn beef sandwiches, fruit buns and a rare luxury, chocolate digestive biscuits provided by Rita's mother. The rare party atmosphere masked underlying currents of animosity from some present but in the here and now fate seemed at last to be smiling on Rita and Brian who shyly held hands and were so nervous they couldn't eat a thing. Although the afternoon party went well the future was by no means certain. But for the present what could have well been a funeral wake now held all the promise of a springtime wedding in the New Year.

"It was, after all, God's Will" said the priest with a smile to muted nods from some of those gathered.

"Amen to that!" said Tony proudly, remembering the trauma of that dreadful night and a two family tragedy that was avoided only in the nick of time.

The Old Oak

Sometime before she was fully awake Sandra realised that it was going to be one of those exquisite sunlit mornings she could remember from childhood. It was exactly like that on the morning which started a day she would never forget. First to rise as usual she relished the early morning time alone which, weather permitting, she would spend in the garden. Warmed by the rising May time sun, a mug of coffee in hand, it was towards the old oak tree that Sandra made her way. It was cool on the rustic seat beneath the spread of the ancient giant where the sun had not yet reached but she stayed there despite the chill. She often talked to the tree in times of stress and found solace in its shade even when branches were bare in Winter. It was as if the tree understood her feelings and by its presence comforted her. This particular morning Sandra was troubled in her mind but her household duties soon intruded on her reverie and she hastened back to the house and the kitchen.

Breakfast was a hurried affair with Nathan snatching a brief glance at the mail between gulps of coffee and mouthfuls of marmalade toast. He seemed preoccupied with work matters and their token good-bye lacked tenderness. Suddenly she was alone again with the solitary day stretching ahead of her. Lately, to her mounting distress, Nathan, her husband of barely two years, seemed to be growing apart from her. The romance of the early years of their courtship and marriage appeared to be a distant almost forgotten dream.

She leaned forward on the edge of the kitchen sink and through the window her gaze roamed the length of the garden where it was caught and held by movements in the old oak. The huge crown of the tree stirred in the breeze, its outermost leaves fluttering for a moment, matching her anxious heart beat. It was as if it were calling to her.

The sunshine drew her outside again and she gathered some succour from the silky green of the lawn and the vibrant colours of the flower borders. Around her as she strolled she was aware of the birdsong and the buzz of insects on the apple blossom and the occasional butterfly that strayed across her path but they did little to raise her melancholy mood.

When she sat beneath the oak, enfolded by the tree's leafy curtains, a brooding sense of doom enveloped her. She began to shiver, but not just with the coolness of the shade. A dark foreboding surfaced in her mind. After a while she could tolerate the feeling no longer and she slumped back against the bark of the tree for relief and wept floods of tears. She cried aloud like a child asking for help.

The oak willed her to be calm. It wrapped her in its spirit tendrils and hushed her into a soothing quiet. This woman was special to the oak. It knew that she thought only of it in terms of the comfort of its shelter and the nuance of the restfulness it extended to her. But this tree had an agenda of its own and was more than merely a compassionate presence. The wisdom of its experience spanned hundreds of years back to the acorn from which it sprang. It had learned much over the centuries of growth as it increased in size and spirit power.

The mighty strength of the ancient oaks had been fostered in many years of fierce competition with other trees to achieve dominance over this land. Thereafter it was the forests of oak that covered the country.

With the coming of people there had been the annual trauma of coppicing which proved to be a blessing since it toughened their roots and gave the oaks an immovable hold on the earth. This oak used its developing robustness of spirit to deter deer from eating its bark and instead welcomed small birds and squirrels which enhanced its popularity with village folk.

But it was when the witches came of a night time to cast their spells beneath its branches that it learned of the dark forces these hags let loose. After the witches were hanged from its boughs by pious churchmen, it was said the oak digested not only their flesh but their evil spirits as well. Now its purpose knew no bounds.

When the woodmen came to cut down the oak to make charcoal they were believed to have been simply consumed by its ever growing hunger. Later the locals said there were others. Lost children, abandoned in the woods, who slept on the bed of its leaves never to awaken. Lovers who sought privacy and sanctuary beneath its mantle and disappeared without trace. Seemingly all had been entombed and devoured by its massive roots.

Returning to the house Sandra felt so drained that all she could do was to collapse into the soft cushions of the settee and drift in a relaxing doze. It was pleasant in the old sitting room with the blackened wood ceiling beams and the Georgian period stone fireplace. She recalled nostalgically how excited she and Nathan had been when they first viewed the house and how overjoyed they were when their offer was accepted and it was theirs to cherish, alongside their special love for each other.

The garden in particular had enchanted her and she fell in love at first sight with the huge oak tree that stood at the far end of the lawn. The sight of the magnificent tree had evoked memories of stories her father told her of his experiences in Africa where it was believed that every tree had a living spirit. He'd explained to her that the native people revered the tree spirits and would placate them with offerings of food and gin, sometimes with blood sacrifices. When she sat beneath the huge spread of the oak and listened to the fluttering of its leaves in summer and the creaking movements of its branches she could feel the living potency of this mighty tree.

As she lay thinking about the house and the garden her mind was suddenly jolted back to the present by the ringing of the telephone, jarring her already tense nerves. When she nervously answered she could hardly believe her ears. It was Nathan and his voice sounded more like the Nathan she loved. Incredibly he asked her to meet him for lunch at the Bridge Hotel in nearby Normington. "If I'm there first I'll wait for you on the seat by the river opposite the hotel" he said. "Take a taxi darling. I'm dying to see you." "I'll be there as soon as I can" she cried breathlessly into the phone. "Wear your summer dress, the one with all the flowers, my favourite if you remember." "Yes, yes I do remember. Oh Nathan I love you so." "I love you too darling. More than ever." The conversation ended. Flushed with excitement she whirled around the room in joyous abandon. Glancing at the clock she noted that it was only five minutes past nine. He must have rung her the moment he arrived at work. Now where was that dress?

Over two hours later she got out of the taxi at the top of the hill so she could enjoy the stroll down towards the river that ran by the hotel. Dressed in her best frock she felt very young again. The light silky fabric hugged her slim frame like gossamer, enhancing her femininity. At that moment a summer breeze brushed her face and stirred her blonde hair. As she drew nearer to the river it sparkled in the sunlight just as she always liked it. Then she noticed the oddly familiar figure of a man on the seat by the bridge but the heat haze made it difficult to see clearly. Was it just her imagination or had that seat been empty just moments before? Shielding her eyes with her hand from the sun she stared ahead and her heart leapt within her breast. All doubts dispelled, it was Nathan waving eagerly to her.

Breaking into a shaky run she hurried towards him as fast as her high heels would permit. She thought how smart Nathan looked as he came sharply into focus and moved to meet her. Then with a broad smile he took her in his arms and all her worries were swept away in the bliss of the moment.

Nathan had booked the table they always had, the one in the corner by the window which looked across the terrace towards the river. He'd brought her a bunch of flowers, long stemmed yellow roses to match her hair he'd said. She almost swooned with happiness as she inhaled their scent. Lunch was perfect, especially since Nathan had ordered a bottle of the best champagne. "To celebrate us" he smiled in answer to her enquiring look.

After they'd eaten they sauntered over the bridge and stopped to gaze at the river. All too soon it was time to leave. Swinging her around Nathan kissed her on the mouth. It was such a gentle loving kiss that the memory of it stayed with her all afternoon. She waved goodbye as he walked away only suddenly to vanish from sight. She vaguely wondered how he had disappeared so abruptly, almost in the blink of an eye. "It must be the effects of the champagne" she chuckled to herself. He probably parked the car behind the hotel she thought as her taxi arrived.

Back home she reflected on how it had turned into a wonderfully happy day. Then she began thinking about how she would plan a special romantic evening when the doorbell rang. Wondering who could be calling unexpectedly, she hurried along the hallway where she could just make out two dark figures silhouetted against the frosted glass door panels. She swung back the door to be confronted by two uniformed police officers and her heart skipped a beat.

The police woman asked if they could come in and ignored her anxious questions until they were all seated. It was the Inspector who spoke first. Soft voiced he asked her to verify her name. Then with an audible sigh he told her that sadly her husband, Nathan John Baxter, had been killed in a road traffic accident early that morning. Her throat constricted and she felt she was choking as she collapsed back into her chair. As his words sunk in she at last found her voice. "You said this MORNING?" she croaked. "Yes Madam, it happened before nine. We couldn't tell you earlier because the crash wreckage hampered our efforts to identify him" he added. "But that's impossible" she cried out hysterically only to find a numbing coldness overwhelm her as the officer shook his head. "These are your husband's are they not?" he said with a gentle finality as he laid Nathan's scorched wallet and battered watch before her on the coffee table. "But we had lun...." she protested as the tears began to flow. The police woman reached out to comfort her as she began to shake and tremble. "So who was there with me" she sobbed distantly as the realisation started to take hold on her mind. A sudden awareness of the day's events caused her to lose control totally and she started to scream and scream with the terror of it all. Mercifully she fainted. A police doctor sedated her and her parents, who lived in Scotland, were informed and asked to come and stay with her. The officers remained with her until she calmed down and then left only at her insistence.

Much later after the police had gone and dusk was darkening the sky she heard someone calling her name from outside. She crossed wearily to the window and looked out. Dimly through the mist of her tears she saw something stir in the twilight down by the old oak. Beneath the tree she made out a shadowy but vaguely familiar figure of a man. To her horror he seemed to be beckoning her to join him.

When her parents arrived the next morning, having driven through the night, they found the house empty. The kitchen door to the garden was wide open but of Sandra there was no sign. They were mystified and searched everywhere for their missing daughter. A more intensive police search over the next few days failed to elicit any indication of her whereabouts.

In the Autumn the oak tree produced a plethora of fine acorns, more than it had ever produced before. After a while a young couple bought the house and the young woman remarked to her partner how exquisite it was to have a magnificent oak tree at the bottom of their garden.

The Legend of The Red Cat

This tale I came across in several rustic bars, heard fragments from country gentlemen who had managed the land and heard whispered gossip amongst domestic staff in a local stately home. I heard diverse variations of the theme but they all involved a particular large feral cat of exceptional renown, a cat which was as red as the sunset and as clever as a gypsy poacher. Here is the unabridged version.

The night was pitchblack in Stag Wood. Starlight could not penetrate the thick foliage overhead and without moonlight to lighten the way between the trees the darkness covered all things in a blackened shroud. All was quiet and nothing moved but the birds and animals were uneasy. Fear had taken hold. There was a presence which was disturbing the tranquillity of the woodland. It was man and he was watching everything. The wood was a place of watchers but this was different. This watcher was dangerous.

Sitting alone in the darkness waiting to catch a poacher was nothing unusual for Tom MacAllaster. It was part of the routine of his life as a gamekeeper but he would never be welcomed by the creatures of the wood because he carried death with him in his jagged steel traps and sickly poisons, which caused a wretched lingering death, but more especially in the instantly lethal discharge of his shotgun. The focus of his watchfulness this night was slightly different from the usual for it was not a man, a poacher, he was waiting to catch but an animal, an especially clever animal which had plundered his Lordship's young pheasant flocks to an alarming degree over the last few months. He was waiting for the appearance of a cat, a solitary big red cat with a genius for subterfuge. The problem of dealing with the cat was complicated because his usual methods of dealing with predators was not working. His tools, the traps and poisoned bait, had failed to snare the cat which had proved to be a shrewd and crafty adversary. Traps had been sprung with impunity and seemingly casual disregard for their fatal peril whilst poison bait had been left covered in cat faeces as a supreme insult to mankind's ingenuity. But now the problem had reached grave proportions. One of her Ladyship's dogs, a Jack Russell puppy, had eaten some of the poison whilst being taken for a morning romp and the animal was seriously ill and even likely to die. Her Ladyship was heartbroken and the order had come down from the Mansion that no further traps or poison bates were to be set for the present. Which begged the question of how to deal with the marauding cat? Hence the gamekeeper's uncomfortable night vigil alone in the woods.

"See if you can shoot the damn thing and let that be an end to it!" And that had been his Lordship's final order of the day. But of the cat there was no sign and in the first light of a cold dawn MacAllaster made his weary way home to the dismay of his wife who knew he had yet a full day's work ahead of him.

⁂

In a cragstone hollow high on the steep side of an abandoned quarry Red Cat was sleeping the morning away. On the stony ledge before him pheasant feathers stirred in the wind that always frequents these high places. They were all that remained of the midnight feast that now filled his stomach with the contentment only an excellent meal can bring and foster blissful slumber. A master of stealth he had scented the man hidden by the stream in the stand of willows and had drunk his fill within easy reach of the shotgun's kill zone but no one heard him and nothing saw him except the little owl scanning the woodland's leafy carpet for rodents. The cock pheasant had been easy to take from his roost in a hazel bush. A shock pounce and a quick snap of his jaws and the plump bird was his. At three years old he was in his prime and relished the wild freedom of his life. He was aware of the dangers he faced each day, his mother had taught him well. A tortoiseshell tabby she had spirited away her red kitten to a safe lair in the craggy hillside when the farmer began culling the number of cats over-running the farm and her litter of five was threatened. As a kitten his looks were exceptional. His fur was red not ginger and his head was large denoting the big cat he would later become. Around his mouth he sported a white smear which resembled a moustache and gave his face a dashing and roguishly debonair look. Snow white socks on all four paws and a huge plumed tail gave his form the undeniable stamp of the pedigree from somewhere back in his ancestry. But it was his eyes that essentially marked him out with distinction, they were amber coloured with bright gold flecks. A more impressive animal the area had never seen and he was to prove his mettle as a supreme hunter amongst a whole colony of predators. He effused an air of nobility about him and among tom cats non ranked higher. He was the sole survivor of the litter and so gained the advantage of having his mother all to himself. He thrived and as he matured the living was easy on the game preserve of his Lordship's estate.

One day he learned a remarkable lesson. He was chasing a young rabbit along the edge of a corn field when there was a strange snapping sound and the rabbit was flung high in the air screaming in pain. As he crept nearer he saw that the rabbit was held fast by something despite its struggles. It was the first time he'd seen a steel trap and subsequently as he encountered more of them concealed in the ditches by the hedgerows and fields he saw what they could do to the animals they trapped. By chance one day when he was prowling around he almost stepped onto one when a gust of wind tossed a broken branch down in front of him and on top of the trap which he hadn't seen. As it sprung it jumped about with the recoil like something alive. It frightened him so much that he spent time sniffing around it but he dared not touch it. He'd seen bloodied paws held in these traps and now he knew that a tree branch could set them off. He also detected the man smell that meant danger. There after whenever he came across a trap he tried to spring it by pushing a twig or a fallen branch onto it. Once as he pushed a branch towards a trap the branch moved a stone which sprang the trap. In this way he learned to overcome the menace of traps which were set specifically to catch him as his reputation as a hunter began to cause alarm. The other thing, the poisoned bait presented no challenge for him only the disgust it created in his fine nose for smells; the man smell was also strong there albeit disguised by the game meat. To overcome the smell he would urinate and sometimes defecate on the obnoxious things. In this way he grew to be a wise cat and as his prowess as a hunter improved attempts to eradicate him by the guardians of His Lordship's Shooting Estate intensified.

Tom MacAllaster met together with the other estate workers for the weekly morning briefing with his Lordship. The good news was that Her Ladyship's puppy was recovering and was expected to regain full health.

"Any progress in hunting down that red cat?" his Lordship barked. Tom could only shake his head and apologise. "Well, the Ridgemount Hunt will be riding at the weekend and with luck he'll be taken along with the foxes. Damn nuisances they are!"

"Take your assistant young William here along with you MacAllaster and see if you can dig up a fox cub or two to whet the appetite of the hounds. Sir Thomas Philby, the Hunt Master, will be more than appreciative if you do and I owe him a favour."

"Very well you Lordship, we'll do our best" said MacAllaster dutifully doffing his cap in respect as he took his leave and with that the meeting ended and the men dispersed to their various duties.

Red Cat awoke with the first rays of the dawn as they stroked the sleep from his face and eyes. Today he would roam and hunt far across his domain and with his first deep breaths of fresh country air he began the new day with a full arched body stretch that only cats can do really well. With mounting hunger he set off on a prowl to find breakfast. Here and there as he traversed the grassy banks and meadows he noticed spots of rumpled turf where a fox had rushed and killed a partridge brooding on her nest. Scattered egg shells bore testimony to the ensuing feast. Further along bent grass stems evidenced where the dog fox had cleaned his teeth running thick stems of grass through his mouth and an untidy clump of feathers where the fox had plucked a hen before consuming the carcass. Later Red Cat cautiously circled a badger den and stopped to sniff fresh deposits of stripped rabbit skins which was their practice before eating the flesh. A pile of fresh earth marked the patch where the badgers had dug into the rabbit burrow. Across from a ditch and in sight of the farm a scuffed plot indicated where during the night a barn owl had decapitated a pheasant and made off with her prey to feed two fast growing owlets. In the early morning a jackdaw had discovered the favoured delicacy and eaten the pheasant brains. Just as the Red Cat's hunger reached urgency level he pounced on an unwary field mouse and relished his first meal of the day. With only a wandering agenda in mind he continued to prowl through copses and ditches startling birds and frogs, meandering along river banks to pause and watch a pair of otters at play and exploring small stream tributaries where the flashing forms of fish caught his eyes until around midmorning he settled to hide in the deep dry verge of a grassy knoll which afforded him a clear all around. He stretched full length, made two full turns then curled his body into a tight ball, closed his eyes and drifted into a restful catnap. It was well he relaxed because soon he would need all his strength to escape from the danger of being eaten alive.

The Red Cat awoke suddenly unsure what had awakened him. He listened intently. A faint sound far off disturbed him and sent his heart racing but he couldn't quite work out what it was but he felt afraid. The sound grew closer and the shock realisation of what it was made the fur on his body stand up and for a moment he was rigid with terror. Now he heard it loud and clear. It was the baying of hound dogs following a scent and the trail they were following seemed to be his. All at once he started running and he fled for his life. He streaked across a wide open field that seemed to go on for ever and as he ran he was suddenly joined by a fox and for a time they ran desperately alongside each other until the fox veered away and made for a wood. Red Cat was tiring now. Cats don't normally run long distances like foxes and wolves. They run in short spurts when they have to but are more accustomed to prowling along and then making a dash to catch something. But this was different. The hounds were gaining on him. He could feel them closing in and there was also the sound of horses galloping. Abruptly Red Cat came upon a stream bed of swift swirling water and he raced up its length until it ended in a waterfall. He stopped, panting for breath and feeling exhausted. Then he remembered one time with his mother when he was still barely a kitten and they had found themselves surrounded by men and dogs on a pheasant shoot. His wily mother had then led him up stream to a waterfall and urged him through the falling water to a safe hide out behind. Frantic to escape the hunt he now pushed his way through the cascade to a soaked ledge of rock within the waterfall itself. At the end of his tether he lay down and drank thirstily from little pools of water around him. Then he watched with nerves twitching as the hounds arrived. He watched them through the opaque window of falling water as they circled around outside. Hardly daring to breathe he remained still inside the dark recess safe behind the plunging waters of the fall. He could see them but they could not see him. A man on a horse seen dimly appeared and whipped the dogs away and for a long time Red Cat could still hear them albeit faintly as they bayed in pursuit of another scent. He remained hidden until after dark and then he emerged wet and shivering. It had been a close run thing and he had found refuge behind the waterfall only in the nick of time. He retraced his path cautiously under the light of a wan half-moon and the strident calls of a little owl as he tracked back to the safety of his den high up in the quarry.

The Monday morning briefing of the men with his Lordship was in full swing. His Lordship singled out Tom and his assistant William with a special mention for providing the Hunt Master with two fox cubs for his hounds. The arrangement had fostered excellent relations between His Lordship and the Hunt Master who was a powerful voice at the Masonic Lodge and could smooth many a path for his friends. After the meeting as they were walking back to the Keeper's Sheds young William voiced his concern over the fate of the fox cubs.

"It don't seem right what we done there, Tom!" he said. "It were cruel and unnatural!" Tom MacAllaster paused a moment before replying.

"Well lad if you start calling what's traditional ways of working countryside cruel then you need to realise that Nature itself is full of cruel goings on between the wild things. Like when a weasel takes a live rabbit by the throat and sucks its blood 'til it dies. Like when a fox gets into a chicken roost and the bloodlust makes it kill them all or when a crow pecks the eyes out of a new born lamb or when a sparrowhawk on the wing kills a blue tit which is feeding nestlings that will now starve to death. That is natural lore."

"But humans are supposed to be above that," William countered.

"What you need to understand Will is that we have to manage the land and strike a balance between caring for the countryside and making a living from it and therefore we need to control what happens on his Lordship's Estate for all our benefit. If the Hunt did not cull the fox population the whole of the Estate would suffer serious consequences. This is the traditional way of country life that has been worked out over countless years for the better."

Wild Adventures in Time and Place

"So feeding live fox cubs to bloodhounds doesn't bother you at all Tom; is that right?" the young man persisted angrily."

"Not wishing to prolong the argument Tom simply smiled and said "Not a bit of it. I can't afford to let it."

"Well then God help you and forgive you!" said William.

"I expect that God needs to forgive and bless us all, Will. Now let's see to those pheasant pens." And with that the talk ended and the real work of the day began.

∽

Red Cat awoke to a day of drizzling rain that was soaking the air and the earth. He felt drained of energy after the trauma of the previous day and was in no way inclined to venture out from his comfortable den. He needed to recuperate and so in the way of cats he started to give himself a thorough tongue wash which among cats is a proven pick-me-up. Afterwards he felt much better and contented himself further by slumbering the rest of the day away. Around midnight pangs of hunger stirred him into taking a prowl. The sky was clear and the rain had stopped but the land was sodden. On the outskirts of the farm he caught a broody red hen which had escaped from the domestic flock and had already laid some eggs. He ate the eggs first and was starting to tear feathers from the hen's body when he found he had company. Across from him in the gloom of the semi-darkness he could just make out two luminous green eyes calmly watching him. It was a young she cat from the farm. Surprisingly he didn't growl at her or chase her off and although pre-occupied with his meal he began to feel a warm glow caused by her presence near him. A shaft of light from the rising moon revealed her in all her feminine appeal. She had body fur the colour of rustic oak leaves in autumn with lines of cinnamon against the dark brown of her head and chest. She had all the feline attributes of grace and elegance and Red Cat was smitten right through to the core of his being. Affecting an inviting pose he shared his catch with her and from those early moments of romancing and courtship the two were ultimately bonded in love. For the next few days which merged into a week of time and then some more, Red Cat experienced the most supreme earth-shattering time of his life. It was a momentously happy union as both cats were enraptured with life together and as they blissfully played their mating games their spirits soared.

In the course of time the pair were seen together and the lines of paw tracks alongside each other noted. When MacAllaster got wind of it an idea began to form in his mind. He thought to himself that since the red cat had coupled himself with a she cat then he wasn't a loner anymore and that made him vulnerable. Red Cat was in love. "This might just be the opportunity I've been waiting for to put paid to that rogue." MacAllaster exclaimed. He devised a plan which involved baiting several 'live' box traps sometimes used to catch red squirrels when it was necessary to move them to a new area. "With the cat's mind on other things we might just strike lucky" and so, with the help of his assistant Young William, several of the traps were laid down in places where the two cats had been observed together. MacAllaster was banking on the fact that the box trap would be new to the red cat's experience and sheer curiosity, for which cats were renowned, might lead to his undoing. Several days and nights passed without any of the traps being sprung although the bait was taken from one of them but Mac Allaster suspected mice had been the culprits. More than a week went by without result and when it seemed that the ploy had proved a failure one of the traps caught a cat only it wasn't red cat it was his mate the tortoiseshell coloured she cat. MacAllaster's initial disappointment at the unexpected development soon turned to anticipation as he concocted a new plan which was diabolical in its strategy. He would use the trapped she cat to lure red cat into a set of steel snares that would put paid to him for once and all. The gamekeeper, proud of his plan which he believed couldn't fail, moved the box trap containing red cat's mate to a position close to the work sheds in which was stored all the gear needed for his work. Then he set six new steel traps, Lane's Best Steel Traps that were guaranteed escape proof, in front of the wire strung door through which the she cat could be seen. Lastly he scattered a light covering of straw over the traps.

"Now all I need to do is wait" Tom Mac Allaster said to himself as he hid in the nearest shed and bided his time.

All alone and terrified the imprisoned she cat wailed helplessly to be free. Her cries resounded on the cooling evening air and echoed far and wide over the countryside. Deep inside Stag Wood Red Cat was combing the ground for signs of his mate when a late afternoon winnowing wind blew over the tree tops and carried her calls of distress down to him. He stopped, rooted to the spot as he strained to catch the sound again. There it came once more and the agony in her voice spurred him to action. Now he knew roughly the direction from whence it came and throwing caution to the wind he streaked towards her location. As he came into the vicinity of the sheds he hesitated because he scented the strong man smell there. At the sight of him the she cat whined in despair at her plight and hearing her he raced to her cage. Too late he sensed the danger as the jaws of the traps slammed shut and held him fast by all four paws. On hearing the snap of the traps MacAllaster darted outside and saw with great satisfaction the trapped form of the red cat.

"Gotcha!" he bellowed gleefully and walked over to survey his captive. "That'll put an end to your capers m'lad" he said addressing the rigid shape of Red Cat who neither struggled nor made a sound.

"Now Missy you've done your bit, be off with you. Scat!" he said as he freed the she cat. At liberty again the cat shot away and was soon lost to sight. Meanwhile the gamekeeper walked over to the shed and collected a garden spade. He intended to finish off the red cat at once and have it all done with so he could go home. As he approached the traps the red cat raised his head and looked straight at him. Their gaze locked and held but only for an instant but in that time Tom MacAllaster experienced a sudden sharp pang of emotion. Nevertheless he meant to do what he felt was necessary and he raised the spade high in the air and aimed to whack it down on red cat's head when something inside stopped him. Thrice more he raised the spade and three times he laid it down. He couldn't do it. Muttering a curse he flung the spade aside and stared down at the cat. Mystified at his own reaction he slowly began to realise that the animal lying at his feet was no ordinary creature. Indeed as he looked closer he could see that this was no wretched vermin but something that had an air of nobility about it like the sight of his Lordship's pedigree horses. Flummoxed he removed his cap, scratched and shook his head and knelt down by the side of the captive cat. As he later related to his wife: "Something just come over me."

"What have I done" he murmured to himself. Feelings formerly unknown to him now overwhelmed his senses. "The way I feel I've almost half a mind to set him free 'cepting his paws'll have been smashed by the traps." He noticed that Red Cat wasn't looking at him anymore but was gazing past him at the shadowy shades of the distant hills coloured blue and purple in the fading light and the longing for freedom was deep within his golden eyes.

MacAllaster suddenly felt consumed by remorse so much so he felt the onset of tears stinging his eyes and he hadn't cried since his mother died. He felt he had to do something for the animal and so in a sort of daze he walked over to the shed and half- filled a tin with water from the tap inside. Placing it before the big cat's head he felt an urgent need to get away from what he'd done. Moved by a shaft of compassion he stopped only to drape a hessian sack over the cat's back to ward off the night chill. After locking up the shed he turned to leave but stopped when he saw that the she cat had returned and was licking Red Cat's face and head. This endearing sight was accentuated by the sounds coming from the two cats. It wasn't meows or whines but a kind of hollow whimpering and cooing like the moaning of hedgehogs when they fight but the soft cries made by the cats were more evocative of sorrow and tenderness than aggression. The sounds he heard made the hair stand up on the back of his neck and suddenly unable to take anymore he hastened away.

"Now where on earth have you been this late with your dinner ready and waiting for you these past hours?" was his wife's greeting as he entered their cottage. He said nothing nor would he eat but sat the whole evening puffing away at his pipe and staring into the fire. "He had the look of a man who's seen a ghost" she confided to a neighbour but on the evening in question she said nothing since she knew he would tell her all when it suited him. Whilst he sat ruminating at the fireside his mind recalled a particular Sunday morning when his wife had pressed him to attend the little chapel in the Big Mansion House to hear the sermon of a visiting preacher invited especially by his Lord and Ladyship. Something the preacher said, which at the time he'd regarded as stuff and nonsense, returned now to haunt him. The man had, as MacAllaster remembered it, made a special point of saying:

"Each one of us has within us a piece of the Divine Creator, it is called a soul. Animals also have it according to their place in the system of life. The remarkable thing about this soul is that it has eternal life and cannot be killed. It is the spirit that ennobles us all."

He'd never ever thought that way about animals; they were either useful like Bess his dog or the horses that worked the farm or they were pests and needed to be controlled and sometimes destroyed as vermin. But something had happened to him in connection with that red cat. It was when he had made eye contact with the creature. It had disturbed him then and it bothered him now because he couldn't fathom the meaning of the feelings it had caused him to have.

Long after midnight the she cat abandoned her vigil next to her mate and made off back to her home at the farm to feed and recover from her ordeal. When she moved she could feel a pod of life stirring below her belly and she knew that it was part of her and Red Cat which needed to be kept safe, something to nurture and to cherish from their time together.

Red Cat noted her leaving but the pain had dulled his senses and the agony of not being able to move had spread throughout his body and weakened him. He turned his big head to the east and waited for the sun to come up. It always pleased him to feel the first glow of morning light. A fond memory surfaced despite the torment he felt and he pictured again in his mind's eye the pleasure of one early dawn viewed from the entrance to his den high in the quarry and he recalled then how a faint breeze had stroked the white fur of his chest and brushed his brow with a touch as light as a sunbeam. And with the rising of the sun there had come a swelling chorus of birdsong from the fields below as skylarks winged up into the brightening sky and flew aloft in songful greetings to the new day and the taste of living was good.

Now as the first red and orange streaks of light seeped through the dark horizon and shone on his desperate plight, Red Cat felt the end creeping closer. Blessed relief came like a divine wind with the welcome golden rays that warmed his face and sanctioned his sapped spirit to ease loose from its suffering body and at last slip freely away.

―⁂―

Tom MacAllaster hurried out as soon as he got up to see what might be done for the red cat. Tormented with feelings of guilt he'd thought fancifully during the night that with the help of a Vet it might be possible to save the creature. But Red Cat was dead he could see that and as he hunkered down to look at him he saw that the cat's eyes had remained open and surprisingly had retained a reflection of the golden sunrise. Tom was deeply troubled. The demise of the red cat and his own part in it had drained him emotionally and he was racked with sadness as he undid the cat's mangled paws from the steel jaws of the traps. If anyone had been within earshot they would have heard him utter a series of 'Damn its' as he retrieved the cat's stiffened body and wrapped it in the hessian sack he'd laid over it the night before. With the body of the cat cradled under one arm he picked up the discarded spade and headed towards the woods. His wife caught sight of him through the cottage window and called for him from the open door to come for breakfast but he paid her no heed. About a mile into the forest Tom halted in front of the gamekeeper's hut, a small timbered building with a corrugated iron roof. It was fitted with wheels at one end so it could be moved. Inside it had a rough wooden pallet for lying on, a high backed rocking chair and a wood burning stove for the cold nights spent waiting for poachers. There was also a store of a few blankets and some oil lamps for comfort. Tom had passed many a night cooped up in the hut hoping to snatch anyone taking game illegally. It was a place of comforting memories which is why he had chosen to come here. Near the hut a young larch tree had grown and it was in this spot that he dug a grave four foot deep for the red cat. He felt miserable and was stricken with guilt in ways that he had never imagined possible. He placed the body in the pit he'd dug and before he filled in the grave he looked down at the body and in a choked voice uttered just one word. "Sorry." It was enough and said it all. After the death of the red cat he was never the same man again but fortunately fate had a few changes in store for him.

When he arrived back at the cottage his wife chided him for going off without his breakfast but aware of his fretful mood she let the matter drop. She told him that Will had called with a message that his Lordship wished to see him. Sensing something special in the summons he washed and shaved before setting off for the Big House.

"Ah, Mac Allaster, good to see you man. Well done over that business with the rogue cat. Now you know George Albury, the Bailiff is due to retire to live with his daughter somewhere in the midlands, been troubled with sickness for some time now. Well I wonder if you'd like his job. We need a good man there and there's a cottage, the old Mill Cottage, goes with it. A good show what? What!" And young Will can accommodate your work so what do you say?"

Tom MacAllaster heaved a sigh of relief. This was just what he needed at this moment in time. A move away from the trauma of the last couple of days would give him a new start so that he could put all that behind him.

"I'll be delighted to accept, your Lordship."

"Right then, it's settled. Make the move as soon as you can. See Ben Hocky at the stables about getting help and transport for moving house and we'll have it all settled in time for the Autumn salmon run."

For the first time in many hours Tom felt his spirits lift and he hurried back to tell his wife the good news. In less than two weeks the house move was completed and Tom was engrossed in his work as his Lordship's Bailiff. He had always been attracted to the river as it curled and wended its way like a living entity over the land and through the forest. Many a morning he had been moved, as now, to stop and stare at the simple beauty of sunlit haze hanging like a diaphanous veil over the water, smooth as glass except for a ripple now and then from a trout or bank vole. He would grow to love his work of husbanding the fish, inhabitants of what was to be his domain for the rest of his working life. He knew this land like the back of his hand. In Winter he'd seen with the first fall of snow the normally unseen burrows where rats nested and the game trails of deer and fox that showed up like pathways across the fields. Life and the living of it settled into a tranquil mode for the Mac Allasters and Tom began to feel like his old self until one day he happened to bump into Jack Morrison, the owner of Ryehope Farm. It was market day and Tom was accompanying his wife who was busy shopping around the stalls. The two men greeted each other and indulged some small talk until Morrison mentioned how he'd heard about the rogue red cat and how Tom had put an end to its predations.

"Cost me a bob or two that cat did. Took both my prize cockerels, one after t'other. Anyway it seems he had his way with one of the farm cats and the wife tells me there's a litter in the barn and one of the kittens is a red tom no doubt the spitting image of his dad and likely to give as much trouble when he grows up so you'll be glad to hear that I've lined him up for the chop when I get round to it."

Tom MacAllaster stood stunned at the news and almost without hesitation blurted out "Don't do that! Please don't do that!"

Jack Morrison turned in astonishment as if he hadn't heard right. "What was that Tom?"

"Don't kill the red kitten, Jack. I'd like to have him myself. Promise me you'll keep him alive for me." Tom and Jack looked at each other and there was affirmation in the looks which confirmed what had been said. "Right then" Jack ever the pragmatic man said "You can come and collect him in 'bout two weeks, he should be ready." And nothing more was said by either man but each departed to his own ways with much to think about.

⁓

"Whatever is Bess going to do when you bring a cat into this house Tom MacAllaster?" his wife said on being told the news."

"Bess is an old dog now she'll not cause trouble when she sees that it's my doing," he replied. His wife said nothing but shook her head in consternation. Would she ever understand this man of hers?

As arranged Tom turned up at the farm to collect the kitten. He was greeted by the farmer's wife who was at pains to tell him that the kitten had just been recently weaned and would need gentle feeding, a cinder box to do his business if kept inside and a comfortable place to sleep of nights. She also mentioned in passing that it was an apt time for the kitten to be homed because the mother cat had been run over by a tractor reversing out a barn just the day before yesterday. Then she looked Tom straight in the eye and said harshly

"You take good care of this kitten Tom MacAllaster. He's not to be used as fit fodder for bloodhounds."

Tom blushed and stammered self-consciously that he meant to keep the little creature as a pet. Having got what he came for Tom gave his thanks and bade his goodbyes and hurried away with red cat junior cradled in his arms.

The red kitten bore the quality looks of being no ordinary feline. He had the makings of being an exceptional cat. The refined lineage was evident in the form of his head and chest and in the contours of his back and legs. His tail promised to be a special feature. But for now at six weeks old he exuded all the kittenish attraction of a miniature teddy bear. The golden colour of his eyes gave Tom a momentary shock even though he was expecting them because they were the spitting image of the eyes he'd looked into that night way back when he'd trapped the big red cat. Tom looked him over and loved him at first sight. This tiny creature offered all the possibility of redemption for Tom, something to calm his soul and enable him to justify his working life again.

"No harm will come to this cat if I have anything to do with it" he declared to all and sundry and Tom Mac Allaster was known as a man of his word.

"What's to be his name then?" asked Tom's wife as she sat and stroked the bundle of red fur in her lap.

"I thought I'd just call him 'Red'," said her husband.

"Well he's red sure enough" she said feeding the kitten choice tit bits of chicken breast.

And so it was that red cat's son came to live with the man who'd trapped his father and Tom felt in his heart that he had achieved a sort of cleansing. Some people of course failed to understand what was going on and some others superstitiously thought that MacAllaster had been blighted and cursed by nature for what he had done but overall opinion was that a circle had been squared as many of the estate workers said knowingly.

Eleven o'clock in the morning was the usual time for the domestic workers in the Big House to gather in the cook house for their morning break. It also offered an opportunity for the staff to exchange gossip and keep up with the local news. Fridays were especially looked forward to because, it being the end of the week, cook usually put together some tasty snacks and on this particular morning there was hot buttered scones and treacle griddle cakes on offer which, once word had got out, had attracted a large gathering.

Luke Matthewson the head groom had something special to share.

"I saw something this morning that'd make your hair stand on end" he said silencing the chatter and capturing everyone's attention. It was his responsibility each morning to supervise the exercise of the horses especially his Lordship's stallion known familiarly as The Donohue.

"I seen, and The Donohue saw them too, a pair of cats, one red and t'other all dark colours and they was playing together on the ridge of yonder old quarry."

"What's the wonder of that?" said Wilkins the Head Gardener.

"Well now the wonder is" said Luke reaching for another scone and conscious of his hold on the audience "That they weren't real cats at all but spirits like."

"Well I never" said cook "Spirit cats, whatever next?" and everyone chuckled.

"I know what I seen" blurted Luke defensively, spilling crumbs down his jacket.

"How'd you know they was spirits?" demanded Wilkins cynically.

"Cos they was kind of floating in the air around the top o' that ridge. I could see them clearly in the early light. It were like they was playing and courting together. Gave me quite a turn I can tell you. Spooked The Donohue into a mad gallop and I had no end of trouble getting him controlled."

"Sounds as if it spooked you too, m'lad" queried cook and Luke simply nodded soberly. Some of those who heard it scoffed at the story but Luke's tale resonated with those who had worked a life time on the Estate and had relatives who had worked there before them and who were well aware of numerous spirits of the past who were apt to make their presence felt now and then in mysterious ways.

Eventually the story filtered down by word of mouth and reached his wife who'd heard it from the housekeeper and so it came to the ears of Tom MacAllaster who found that he couldn't shake it out of his head. That night as he sat smoking in his rocking chair by the fireside with Red Cat Junior cuddled into his lap he began to wonder about it. He had recently, with the help of the red kitten, been able to come to terms with the demise of the big red cat. Only a few days back he had taken the kitten, which was growing larger by the day, on a sneak visit to where his sire was buried. When he arrived at the site he was surprised to find the grave under the Larch Tree covered in cowslips which evoked a memory of childhood when his Gran had a saying:

"Where cowslips abound the fairies have blessed the ground."

With no one else about he'd set the kitten down among the cowslips and whilst it chased flies through the grass he addressed the grave

"There now you can see I've tried to make amends and I'll take right good care of your kitten." The remarkable thing is he in no way felt foolish in what he said or in having brought the kitten there.

Now as he pondered on Luke's story he couldn't help muttering out loud:

"No! It can't be."

His wife looked up from her knitting at his words and questioned his meaning. Not wishing to explain he mentioned that he'd seen rabbits feeding early this morning.

"Sure sign of a storm coming," he volunteered. And that night there did come a storm as fierce as ever had been. One gust of wind rattled the windows of the cottage as if they were about to be blown in and set Bess barking her head off. The logs on the fire sparked and began a storm of their own as the draught wailed up the chimney. Red, fast maturing in size with the promise of being a big cat, raised his head from his incumbent position on Tom's lap, pricked his ears and listened attentively to the sounds of the wind which weren't just the wind. He stared fixedly at the door as if there was something outside come calling. His amber eyes glowed and sparkled for a brief moment of understanding, then he laid down content to sleep and dream of cat things.

Tom, still pondering what he'd heard from his wife, mechanically stroked Red's silken fur and stared bemusedly into the embers of the fire'.

"I wonder" he whispered quietly to himself "I just wonder."

The Parson's Kitten

While out walking in the Cheviot Foot hills one autumn day I came upon an old chapel, built in the Jacobean style of times long past. Nearby a wood of vintage broadleaf trees, chiefly oak and ash, afforded shelter from the wind and a sparkling stony brook fronted the sprawl of archaic headstones in the church yard. The studded oaken door to the interior was locked but a stone porch offered sanctuary from the elements. At either side of the porch rough hewn wooden benches offered rest for the weary and I was grateful to sit a while and allow the charm of the setting to enfold me. As my eyes adjusted to the interior gloom some writing carved into the stone above the door caught my eye and fired my imagination. The messages read:

God Bless the Parson the Reverend Enoch Blunkstone

God Bless the Parson's Kitten which has enchanted his Soul

The second line of the prayer jolted my mind with baffled incomprehension. How strange it was that such a message should have been cut into a tablet of stone. All at once the weather outside aroused my attention. A creeping ground mist was enveloping the chapel grounds and coiling around the tree trunks with wreaths of hazy vapour, closing me off from the world beyond the shelter of the porch. The mist cooled the air and I snuggled deeper inside my anorak and was lulled by the warmth into closing my eyes for a blissful respite as I drifted deeply in drowsy comfort. Bit by bit sleep overcame me and with it a flow of images which over whelmed me and brought a dream that took hold of my mind.

There was movement in the unkempt grass fringing the graves. A light grey, some would say silver, she-cat, heavily pregnant, moved into a gap beneath a fallen headstone and went to earth. Soon she would have her kittens here safe from the vixen which had latterly been stalking her in the wild wood. Safe from predators and the prying eyes of the village folk who came to worship. She gave birth two nights later to a litter of twin kittens, a male and a female. Stray moonbeams momentarily illumined the hollow where she nested and brightened the dark interior just sufficiently for her to see the burnished copper coloured fur, etched with white, of her kitttens. Colours inherited from her mate, a feral farm cat. She tongue washed them clean and afterwards, in response to their puny cries, lay on her side so that they could feed from her milk. Outside seasonal shades of autumn saturated the ground with vibrant gold and orange hues. Windfalls of ripe apple and mulberry fruits, succulent fruits of the forest, littered the ground bringing nature's food harvest to the wildlife to enable them withstand the privations of Winter. The air around the Chapel walls resonated with the shrill cries of swallows atop the gable ends, readying themselves for the long migration. Below the brook made soothing music as the whispering breeze shed leaves from the trees. A red sunset stained the West Wall of the Chapel with tints of vermilion and cinnamon and everywhere the fields and the woods were adorned with signs of the earth yielding to autumnal rest.

Underground the kittens thrived until one day, as the cat slipped out on a hunting foray, the ground was hard with frost and a stray snowflake brushed her whiskers alerting her to the imminent danger of winter storms. She would move her vulnerable family to a safer hide, a weathered crevice high in an oak tree deep in the forest. When it was dark she picked up the larger kitten, the female, in her mouth, holding it securely by the scruff of its neck, and headed swiftly along a worn game trail through the trees. She neither heard nor saw the danger as the vixen pounced and with one snap of its jaws broke her neck. The kitten provided a quick meal for the hungry fox after which she hurried away with the body of the cat hanging from her fangs. Her starving cubs would welcome the meal as game in the wood had become scarce since the rabbit population had been decimated by disease. Back at the abandoned nest under the tombstone the remaining kitten grew cold and hungry. He missed the warm comfort of his sister's presence and the succour of his mother's body. He waited anxiously for his mother's return but the waiting became too long to bear. Barely four weeks old his tiny form laboriously scratched and struggled a way up the short tunnel to the surface only to be forced back by a chill wind gusting across the graveyard. Crouching in the opening he began to shiver and with the shivering he cried, shrill forlorn cries of desperation snatched away on the wind.

The Rev. Enoch Blunkstone was early to bed. He was reading by candle light from the candelabrum by his bedside. There was a blanket around his shoulders to fend off the cold air and he wore woollen gloves to protect his hands from the cold as he held a book up to his face to read. The windows rattled in the draught from the gap under the door and the bed springs creaked whenever he moved accentuating the bareness of the old fashioned bedroom. Tired of reading he closed his book with a bored sigh and, extinguishing the candles, lay down to sleep.

Strange it is, he thought to himself, how darkness amplifies the faintest sounds, like the creak of the door latch jerked by the wind as it whistled through the empty corridors of the manse. But it wasn't the door latch that alerted the sharp ears of the Parson as he lay dozing, it was the almost inaudible wail outside of an animal in distress.

Fumbling in the darkness to relight the candles he heard the cry again and yet once more in the stay of the wind as he made his way downstairs wearing only his night gown and slippers and the woollen blanket draped like shawl around his tall but slight frame. Contrary to his usually stern, even forbidding facial expression, Parson Blunkstone was an earnestly caring man and, quite apart from his small congregation, he cared for every living creature in his Parish. He had built a reputation for kindness and caring which he extended not only to people but also to the wildlife he encountered in this rural idyll. An astute observer, noticing the soft hazel colouring of his eyes, could understand the stories told of how he would go to extraordinary lengths to accommodate injured birds and wounded animals.

On hearing the wail of distress he was unable to sleep any further and was moved to venture forth despite the darkness and the cold to minister to something obviously needing help. That was how he was made and how he was with everyone and everything.

Standing at the front door of the Parsonage he contemplated what to do next. The cry came again, the sound faintly on the wind as if it were becoming increasingly hopeless. Conscious of the frailty of life the Parson was impelled to move. Donning a thick black serge overcoat over his nightshirt and carrying an iron oil lantern he set out into the Chapel grounds. Frustrated at being unable to identify the source of the wails he was about to surrender to the freezing night air when he spotted a slight movement. Lowering his lamp to ground level he peered closely at a gap underneath a fallen gravestone. The hole was thrown into sharp relief by the white frost on the pathway and barely visible was a tiny whiskered face and two minute pointed ears framed within the darkness of the opening. As the light lit up its face the kitten repeated the anguished wail that had alerted the Parson to mount a midnight rescue. Surprised that such a small creature could cry so loudly, he carefully gathered up the little mite, which on contact with his warm hand, began to shiver feverishly. Setting down the lamp he knelt and explored the cavity with his free hand to ascertain if there were any others inside. Finding nothing he stood up with the kitten still nestled in his hand but as he raised the lamp he became aware of something watching him. He turned and holding the lamp head high he was confronted by a fox, the same vixen which had killed the mother cat and her kitten. Having fed her cubs she had doubled back to track down where the cat had nested to check if there were any remaining kittens. As fate would have it the kitten now safely in the hands of the Parson had escaped death only in the nick of time. Fearful of the delicate state of his foundling the Parson, ignoring the fox whom he suspected had been attracted by the kitten's cries, hurried back to the security of the Manse.

Once indoors he wasn't sure what to do next. The kitten was now suffering a spate of shivering and something would have to be done. The huge expanse of the kitchen seemed bleak and lacked the usual warmth generated by his housekeeper, Mrs Edwards. And then he recalled an incident from his youth when studying at the Seminary.

He quickly recollected it now. It was Winter and the nearby lake was frozen affording himself and his fellow students a rare opportunity to have some fun as they skated around with uproarious merriment until the ice broke near the shallows and several of them, including himself, received an icy dunking. He called to mind how desperately cold he had felt and how it was only after a warm bath that his fits of shivering were alleviated. Perhaps a warm bath would relieve the kitten which was still trembling. Retrieving his large felt parson's hat from the hall he placed it upside down on the kitchen table and gently placed the kitten inside. At least the hat would give the tiny creature a measure of comfort until he could prepare a bath. Then he ignited the gas ring on the top of the cooker and placed a pan of water to heat. It didn't take long before the water was bubbling by which time he had found a white enamel pudding dish in one of the cupboards. Filling the dish with water from the pan he tested it with his hand and felt it would be just right. Tenderly he immersed the kitten in the reviving water. The soothing effects of the bath were immediately apparent as the little cat opened its eyes and relaxed in the healing warmth. "Good idea Enoch" he murmured to himself as he watched with relief the frozen kitten becoming reanimated. Hunting for and finding a fluffy towel he removed the kitten from the bath and placing it on the towel he slowly rubbed it dry with caring hands. On examining the kitten's body for any injuries he saw that it was a male.

During these ablutions the kitten never uttered a sound but now, snug and dry, with its fur all fluffed out it formed a most endearing pose as it sat on the table. To his surprise it suddenly raised its head and looked directly at him. It would possibly be far-fetched to say there was gratitude in the kitten's gaze but there was a positive emotional connection shining in two bright blue eyes. The Parson smiled down at the kitten with affection and softly stroked its knob of a head. He felt impelled to address the kitten almost as if he were speaking to a person. "You were left alone and about to suffer death in the fangs of a fox. I do believe there was something like divine intervention in your stay of execution and therefore I shall call you Jacob after a kinsman of mine who was also only saved from an English firing squad by the wily intervention of a minister of the cloth." All at once the wee animal uttered a soft whimper and lay down folding its legs beneath its body in a manner that could only be described as expectant.

"Of course!" the Parson exclaimed, smiting his forehead "The creature is hungry!" Galvanised into action he searched the kitchen. There were the remains of yesterday's milk amounting to about a quarter of the bottle and "Aha" he exclaimed as he discovered an open jar of honey. Mixing a tea spoonful of honey in a cup of heated creamy milk he stirred the concoction until it thickened. But how to administer the mixture to the hungry kitten perplexed him at first. Then he had a brainwave. Bounding up the stairs, his rapid steps making a noise like thunder on the bare staircase, he retrieved a new linen handkerchief from a drawer in his bedroom. Swiftly returning downstairs he made a spear of the cloth which he then dipped into the mixture he had prepared. Holding the kitten firmly in his left hand he stroked its mouth with the soaked fabric. After an agonising wait the kitten opened its mouth and licked the residue of milk left around its muzzle. With repeated applications the kitten sucked and licked the milky food until its diminutive appetite was sated. Much relieved that his efforts had succeeded he quite suddenly felt very tired. Now that the kitten had some sustenance in him he suddenly surprised the Parson by commencing to do a very cat like thing. True to his feline nature he immediately set to, with a bright red tongue to wash himself. The Parson was fascinated and momentarily all thoughts of sleep and bed were put side as he marvelled at the resilience of the tiny being before him. Defying the adversity of recent life events the kitten was now showing the independent streak that characterises all cats by doing his own thing. "Jacob is obviously going to be quite a personality" mused the Parson as he wondered where he was going to leave the kitten for the rest of the night. Then he thought of the reaction his housekeeper might have in the morning if she unexpectedly came upon a kitten in the kitchen. Uncertain what to do and suddenly feeling yet another wave of tiredness he decided that he might as well just take the kitten up to the bedroom with him. Ensconced once more in his large rickety bed the Rev. Blunkstone was dismayed to find that the kitten was not happy to stay in the shoe box lined with tissue paper he had prepared for him but was mounting a valiant attempt to climb out, which due to his size was proving a feat beyond his capability. At the same time, the kitten was emitting the identical piercing wail which had alerted his rescuer in the first place. The matter was only resolved when the Parson surrendered to the inevitable compromise of allowing the kitten to stay on the bed, albeit between the counterpane and the blanket. Calm at last descended upon the manse and in the bedroom overlooking the graveyard two bodies slept in the tranquillity that only deep slumber can bring. It was almost four in the morning too soon even for the cockerel at Windy Edge Farm to begin his clarion call. The vixen was back in her den resting with her cubs and all creatures inhabiting the wild wood were dormant even the bats had returned to their roosts after the night's foraging. The sky was dark except for a fading quarter moon and a hoar-frost coated the ground in an iced white sheen. The wind had died and nothing further disturbed the serenity that night.

When Mrs Edwards arrived next morning she was shocked to find the kitchen in a mess. Splodges of milk and splotches of sticky honey stained her clean oakwood table. Cupboards were ajar and the pantry was wide open. One of her pie dishes bore a residue of dirty water and hairs. "What a shambles!" she exclaimed so loudly that the Reverend Enoch Blunkstone was rudely jolted awake. The events of last evenings flooded back to his mind and in some alarm he cast his eyes around for the whereabouts of the kitten. A bulge in the surface of the counterpane indicated a presence beneath. When the bedspread was folded back it revealed a curled body of silky fur that was just beginning to awaken. Jacob the kitten was still somewhat sleepy but now stretching and yawning he was nonetheless ready to start life anew. Meanwhile the Parson, after a quick wash from the basin in his bedroom, briskly dressed and descended the stairs to 'face the music.'

Downstairs Mrs Edwards was still stridently complaining about the state of her kitchen and the Parson was at pains to mollify her. He explained to her that last night had presented him with an emergency situation and that he had barely been in time to rescue a young kitten. On learning that the kitten was now upstairs on his bed she further remonstrated with him about the problems of having an animal in the house. She advised him to leave the kitten with her and she would find a home for it in the village. Presented with this ultimatum the Rev. Blunkstone's resolve stiffened in a way his housekeeper had not previously seen. He faced her sternly and stated that he had no intention of getting rid of the kitten but that he was determined to keep it as a pet. Somewhat taken aback by his unusually adamant manner Mrs. Edwards frowned but made no reply which was just as well because at that precise moment a cute little personage with the imposing name of Jacob presented himself in the kitchen with all the aplomb gifted to the feline species. Uttering a teeny miaow he stared up expectantly at the two adults. The housekeeper was the first to respond. "Well I never did see a more beautiful kitten" she murmured smiling, her manner softening. "And now I suppose you'll be wanting something to eat" she said beaming, "The both of you" she added glancing towards the stiff figure of the Parson who was relieved by the change in her manner. In no time at all it seemed strips of bacon and links of pork sausages were sizzling away in the large black frying pan. But also, no doubt with the kitten in mind, she took two fresh eggs from her shopping bag and whisked them into a bowl of creamy milk to prepare scrambled eggs. Served on fresh baked brown bread for the Parson and on a saucer for the kitten, breakfast was dished up. Gazing over his steaming mug of hot milky tea the Parson was comforted to see Jacob stoutly tackling such new- fangled food and with much licking of his lips managed to clear his dish. He then retired to the warmest place in the room, which was near the wood and coal fired iron stove which the housekeeper had just lit. Once there he commenced to lick wash himself all over as befitted his instinct. Turning to face his housekeeper the Parson was humbly vociferous in his thanks. It was Monday morning at the Manse and everything was turning out very well.

Later in the day the Reverend Blunkstone attended to some work in the Chapel and departing from his normal routine he took Jacob with him. The kitten's presence in the austere church interior rendered his ministering duties a degree of comfort as he kept an eye on the little cat's meandering exploration of the wooden pews and the worn stone flooring. Now and then he lost sight of him only to be surprised by a squeaky miaow from a diminutive ball of fur at his feet. Eventually the kitten did what all cats do when they become slightly bored he sought out a snug place to lie down. When he couldn't find him the parson became unduly alarmed and thinking that he might have fallen down one of the numerous gaps where the floor met the walls he embarked upon an anxious search until he at last discovered him in a sheltered corner of the pulpit.

The Reverend Blunkstone held church services every Sunday morning and evening. Some in the congregation remarked that the tone of his sermons became less harsh and more compassionate sounding since the advent of th cat. Sometimes as he delivered his ecclesiastical homilies church goers were astonished to spot a whiskered face peering out from the foot of the pulpit. Observing their reaction the Parson would beam indulgently before carrying on with his sermonising which never seemed to last as long as previously. But it was the kindly gossip of his housekeeper which most intrigued the village folk. Attending the Manse every day she gained an insider's view of all that went on there. She recounted tales of how the Parson doted on the kitten. They go everywhere together and he talks to him constantly as if he were a relative of his. "More like the child he never had," observed the baker's wife, nodding knowingly. Tom Higginbottom, who did some gardening in the Chapel grounds, often saw the Minister out walking, a tall gaunt figure dressed from head to foot in black wearing his large floppy parson's hat and laced black boots. The gardener could hear the Parson reciting his Office from the book of Common Prayer. This was a regular sight but what intrigued him was the spectacle of the cat following in his master's footsteps. Now and then the Minister would stop, close his prayer book and sit on one of the garden benches. Immediately the cat would hurry across and jump on his knee and the Parson would stroke and talk to him all the while. "Everywhere he went the cat went too, it followed like a little dog." As Tom related to the regulars at the bar of the Red Bull. "It t'were as if they couldn't bear to be separated from each other. Strange it was to see them" he laughed shaking his head.

In the house itself Mrs Edwards was equally bemused by the sight of the Reverend Blunkstone feeding the cat morsels of whatever he was eating for his supper, be it meat or cheese. The kitten called Jacob, now grown to cat size, would lie in the Parson's lap as he composed his sermon in front of a log fire. "I've never seen him so relaxed and pleased with himself since that cat came into his life" she told the neighbours. "He seems a much happier man. It's uncanny, almost as if they were soulmates existing in a different world from the rest of us."

As Christmas approached the Parson erected a crude crib in a corner near the altar containing wooden figures of the Nativity carved by local carpenters. A singular addition to the Holy Family scene during Church Services was the presence of Jacob snoozing among the hay, a feature which caused great hilarity amongst the children.

Every weekday the Parson would take a morning walk, weather permitting, around the garden of the Manse accompanied by his faithful cat. One beautiful sunny morning in early May as he sat on a garden seat he observed that the sky above Cheviot was festooned with high quilted clouds folded like white silk shimmering in the sunlight. A nature lover at heart such pastoral scenes were a delight to him. But on one such morning he confided to Jacob that he felt a premonition that his time on earth would soon be over and his only regret would be leaving him. Jacob licked the back of his hand, purred and looked at him adoringly.

Life at the Chapel Manse proceeded in this contented uneventful way until, in his fifty ninth year, when the cat was three years old, the Reverend fell ill. The illness progressed rapidly to a terminal stage and on a cold windy day in early March the Parson died. All during the period of the illness the cat hardly ever left his side and in the latter stages of the sickness it could be seen in a self- appointed position on the bed watching over the Parson with loving devotion. The cat would purr every time he stroked it and it would frequently reach to lick his hand. The feelings of love and affection were reciprocal. Indeed on the day he died the Parson's hand was seen to be lying on Jacob's body as if even in death they were connected.

The Reverend Enoch Blunkstone was buried three days later in the churchyard he had presided over for the last twenty six years. He had no living family to mourn him and only a few villagers, his housekeeper, the gardener and George the stone mason attended his funeral. Jacob the cat appeared distraught after his death and would wander between the corridors, the kitchen and the bedroom mewing and crying for the Parson. Although he drank from his bowl of water in the kitchen he would not eat despite Mrs Edwards attempts to entice him with customary titbits. Three weeks after the Parson died Jacob disappeared and could not be found. On a Monday morning about a month after the funeral, Tom the gardener was tidying up the graveyard when he spotted the body of the cat lying on the Reverend Blunkstone's grave. Jacob was dead and his body looked emaciated as if it had been out there some time in all weathers. He hastened to tell the housekeeper who appeared quite upset. "Poor thing" she said "It pined for him and could not be soothed." She asked him to bury the cat somewhere in the Chapel grounds since it had a right to belong there as much as anyone.

On the Monday evening Tom met up with George, the stone mason, in the bar of the Red Bull. Over a pint of ale Tom told George about finding the cat on the Parson's grave and how it had saddened him to realise that it had died of a broken heart. "So what did you do?" queried George. "I buried it. I dug a hole four foot down at bottom of Parson's grave. Wrapped the cat's body in a bit of hessian and buried it there. It were only right and proper for them to be together as they were in life. Do you think I done right?" George nodded and added "It was what the Minister would have wanted; he loved that cat as everybody who ever saw them together knew. Mebbe's I can do them some kind of memento like, so they won't be forgotten." "What do you have in mind then?" asked Tom but George only smiled and drew deeply on his pipe.

Several days later the inscriptions appeared on the stone in the porch and on the Parson's grave stone near the top there appeared a newly chiselled outline of a cat. No one commented on these additions, even if they were noticed, for there was a general feeling that it was only right and seemly.

It was dark when I awoke, stiff and numb with cold. I stood up in the porch, stamped my feet and swung my arms to revive my circulation. As I left the earth around the Chapel was just beginning to frost over and it crunched beneath my boots. A full moon lighted my way back to the country road leading to the village. At one stage I felt impelled to look back. The Chapel and the graveyard were bathed in silver moonlight and appeared almost sepulchral.

I had booked a room at Ye Old Red Bull Inn earlier in the day on my way up country. After a hearty meal I joined some of the locals in the bar. After few drinks later in conversation with mine host I asked about the Chapel I had found. "You mean the old ruins among the grave stones?" he volunteered. "Well no; I meant the Chapel." He gave me a queer look then called across to a man he called the Vicar who was part of an animated group clustered in a corner. "This fellow here is asking about the Scots Chapel." A tall clergyman detached himself from the group and came and introduced himself. I lost no time in asking him about the Chapel. "Well I'm not sure what you found. I must admit I haven't been up there lately and the locals tend to steer clear of it because it has a reputation for being haunted. Anyhow it was looted and pillaged a long time ago in the border skirmishes between the Scots and the English. "What did you find out. I believe there are still some interesting ancient headstones?" "Buttttbuttt I saw it" I responded lamely meaning the Chapel. "Well I'm glad you found something of interest in our area. Please excuse me I must rejoin my church committee."

Feeling tired and somewhat confused I finished my drink and bade all goodnight. I slept deeply that night and did not dream at all. The next day after breakfast I set out to find the Chapel again. You know I never did find it either then or ever again despite several later expeditions. When I became a writer I decided to set down what I experienced in my dream. I can only surmise that somehow I was made witness to an episode from the past which powerfully belonged to, and now would for ever, haunt the place as it would my mind.

The Wolf of Fuengirola

Late one evening I sat on the beach fringing the Spanish resort of Fuengirola. Behind me the sun was setting and casting an amber glow in the sky. The sea was calm and the only dominant sound was the mesmeric swish of the waves lapping the sand. As I lazily watched my eyes caught a movement along the beach by the edge of the sea. It was a large animal running and I at first assumed it was a dog. But then something about the way it moved arrested my attention. It wasn't running it was loping, a long bounding stride that effortlessly covered the ground as if it could go on for ever. This was no dog as I was soon to find out. Suddenly the creature turned and headed directly towards me. I straightened up beginning to feel alarmed but before I could move it had closed the distance between us and I came face to face with it. My heart started to pound and I felt the onset of panic as I found myself confronted for the first time in my life by a full grown wolf. In a moment it had swept past me but in that instant I had made eye contact with a beast out of mythology and the source of human nightmares. I will always remember the eyes. Yellow with flecks of black and green and an intensity of stare that was frightening. I turned to see where it had gone and was amazed to observe it waiting on the promenade by the zebra crossing for the traffic to stop. People walking by registered alarmed looks and then hurried past. As the road became clear the wolf crossed the zebra crossing alone and headed purposefully through a gap in the buildings opposite and vanished from sight. I could hardly believe my eyes. My mind began at once to doubt my senses. Had I not simply seen a large German Shepherd Dog or Alsation as they are sometimes called? But my memory of the creature remained sharply clear and I determined to track it down to verify that what I had seen was in fact a wolf wandering the beach and streets of a Spanish coastal town. I did not have to wait long. A few days later on a hot afternoon as I made my way back to the apartment my wife and I had rented, I saw the wolf again. To avoid the heat of the sun I was walking along a shaded side street parallel to the beach carrying a heavy shopping bag. The wolf was suddenly there in front of me. It was lying on the tiled pavement in front of the open door to a small house. When it saw me it sat bolt upright and yawned displaying an awesome jaw full of yellow fangs. I cautiously circled around him and studiously avoided eye contact but I did note the location of the house. When I reached our apartment on the tenth floor I immediately went out on the balcony to check the direction from where I had seen the wolf. I determined to mount a watch later to see if I could observe the creature's movements. My wife amused me by refusing to believe my story thinking that I was just trying to frighten her.

The next time I passed the house where the wolf apparently lived there was no sign of it but a man and a woman were sitting outside taking the air. "Buenos dias" we greeted each other pleasantly enough. On the spur of the moment I smiled and asked in Spanish

"Where is the wolf?"

They both laughed at my question and the man opened his arms and gestured widely speaking in Spanish indicating that 'El Lobo' was gone walkabout. I nodded and went on my way aware that the couple certainly harboured the animal and it intrigued me how that had come about.

As chance would have which it I recognised the man again when my wife and I called into a local bar for a coffee and cognac. We exchanged names. He was called Ramon and his wife Maria. Over a drink and in halting Spanish/English I was able to gather some further information about El Lobo, (The Wolf). At the sound of our loud conversation as we struggled to communicate several others in the bar including the owner joined in our discussion. Whilst my wife listened stoically to my efforts to find out more, I pressed the company for facts about what they were telling me regarding 'The Wild Wolf' issue in Spain. From the conversation in the bar and by my own research later it appeared that the wolves were chiefly active in the mountain ranges linking Italy and Southern France to the Northern Spanish mountains, the Sierra Nevada. But from the conversation in the bar they were far from welcome due to

Wild Adventures in Time and Place

outcries from goat and other livestock farmers living in the area. It is a region of peaks over 300 metres high, where snow lingers until early July and commences falling again in late Autumn and where there is great diversity of rare plants and wildlife such as golden eagles and special butterflies. It seems that here is where the Iberian Wolf is attempting to make a comeback. But there are hazards in store for the re-emerging wolf packs of Northern and North Western Spain. Whilst the government issues annual licences to hunters indicating the quota which can be legally shot, (usually a number around 150), there is widespread poaching and illegal shooting by farmers to protect their livestock in spite of research which shows that wolves prefer a diet of roe deer and wild boar to animals such as goats and sheep. Because of this the wild wolves are in the process of being annihilated. The one factor, however, which emerged from our bar room discussion which may be crucially instrumental in saving the Spanish wolf from extinction is the growing interest from tourism.

I needed to know more about these intriguing animals and so as part of our holiday excursion plans we arranged to visit a special centre where wild wolves were kept in captivity.

A Visitors' Centre in Antequera has a large area where different breeds of wolves are quartered. In September 2009 my wife and I paid a visit to this Lobo Park to see wild wolves for ourselves. We booked a conducted tour which was due to commence sometime after eight o'clock to be led by the owner, Daniel. It proved an experience never to be forgotten. Prior to the tour we sat outside at picnic tables and ate a pre-packed meal provided by the Centre. As the sunset started to take hold of the sky with strikingly colours and layered bands of red, orange and yellow, the wolf packs started to stir and begin their spine-tingling howls. At once the area was psychologically transformed into a wild place dominated by the sound of wolves. A large black dog belonging to the centre slunk out of sight at the racket as the air filled and reverberated with the howling.

Lobo Park has four different enclosures holding subspecies of Canadian Timber, Eurasian, Alaskan Tundra and native Iberian wolves. As one pack began to howl the others tuned in and responded until the whole park resonated with the wolves calling in chorus to each other and to the sky as the silver disc of a moon appeared over the darkening landscape. We joined a small group of enthusiasts, visitors like ourselves being led towards the enclosures. At first sight of us the wolves showed no sign of freaking out mainly due to the fact that they had been raised with the bottle by the owners to acclimatise them to humans. Each of the enclosures supported a natural environment of trees and bushes together with stony outcrops. The Canadian and the Alaskan wolves appeared the most formidable and aggressive. But all the wolves looked fresh and healthy and extremely curious towards us almost as if in greeting. It was interesting to observe how the wolves functioned as an integrated group. This became apparent as they watched us especially the Iberian wolves which were the ones in which I was most interested. They peered at us not singly but as a family and eleven intent faces inspected us. Some of the visitors were disturbed and a little frightened by this scrutiny. As I approached the different compounds I grew aware of a change happening. It was something eerie which vibrated emotionally within me, it felt alien and yet strangely familiar as if deep in my brain there awoke a resonance of kinship with these animals. Primeval images appeared in my mind's eye of grey mountainous vistas under a sky of scudding clouds cloaking a white moon. A pervasive scent of brutish musk hung in the air as bloodlust launched the wolves in a deadly chase. Later there was snarling and the sound of tearing flesh as the wolves ate their meal and I realised that my mind was back in tune with the enclosure as the animals were being fed. For a while an ancestral memory in my mind had merged with reality. Much later there was the howling again which never seemed to stop and which in an odd way soothed me. The excitement and enchantment of the visit stirred a deep fascination in me which remained the focus on my return to the apartment in Fuengirola.

Now whenever I met up with Luis, Ramos and Ramon there were others in the group who also were anxious to share their fund of wolf anecdotes with me. I was drawn compulsively to listen to their tales some of which I had already heard but which continued to captivate me non-theless. Two of the men, strangers I hadn't seen in the bar on the previous occasions, had hunted wolves in the past and had an alarming yarn with an unusual twist to relate. They described an expedition high in the sierras when temperatures were far below freezing and snow storms restricted visibility. The hunters had already achieved contact with a wolf pack and had shot and killed a wolf which was protecting the rear of the pack. Each wolf takes responsibility for protecting the family at all times and the priority of the rear guard wolf is to ensure that nothing can mount a surprise attack from behind as the pack travels along. It was a she-wolf who turned to face the hunters as they closed on the trail of the pack. She barked a warning and stood her ground but was no match for men firing heavy ammunition. At the sound of the shots and the shrill death cries of the she-wolf, the pack scattered for survival. In the aftermath of the shooting the two hunters became lost and failed to link up with the main expedition. Struggling against the harsh weather conditions which were turning everything to ice, guns clothing, and skin, the men strove to find a way down the mountain slopes. It was heavy going and dangerous where compasses were rendered useless and progress could be made only by luck and dead reckoning. Suddenly they grew aware of a scary event happening around them. Scant glimpses through the swirling curtains of snow of dark figures silently circling them. The wolves were closing in,

Wild Adventures in Time and Place

stalking these men who had come to kill them. Roles were being reversed, the hunters were now the hunted. The rest of the trip was an experience never to be repeated and the two men crossed themselves in religious fervour as they repeated their pledge never to go hunting wolves again. They maintained that they were fortunate to escape with their lives because the wolves followed them all the way back to their vehicle.

"They were waiting for us to stop, Senor, to collapse in the snow as their prey do and they would have attacked us with a vengeance. They would have killed us easily because our guns were frozen stiff and we had no means of protection, we were almost finished."

After hearing this account along with many others I began to form an impression of the wolf as a special animal that is not lacking in either intelligence or nobility. I had discovered already that wolves live in packs of eight to ten animals. The leader is an Alpha. Male and his mate is the Alpha Female and they alone can breed. When the pups are born the rest of the wolves act as surrogate parents. The wolf pack is a tightly knit social unit and is renowned for its feral intelligence. When they hunt they move in a coordinated attack which may involve running down prey over long distances. Their only enemy is man. Hunters, using powerful rifles with telescopic sights, have over time achieved a dominance which affords the wolf little chance of escape and perhaps of survival as a species. In some cases organised wolf hunts are conducted by air and the animals are shot from low flying helicopters. When hunters sight a pack they will attempt to wound the alpha bitch which will lead them to the lair where they can kill the pups. The practice is aimed at culling and controlling wolf numbers as a protection for the farmer's livestock but in operation it involves annihilation. Although sympathy for the wolf is traditionally muted to say the least there was a strong feeling voiced in our group for the preservation of the wolf as a facet of national Iberian wildlife. Someone mentioned the necessity for centres where wolves could be kept in natural surroundings for the benefit of tourism such as the one I had recently visited. In essence such a move might be the only means of saving the Iberian wolf from extinction.

Since by most accounts the wolves in Spain appear to be in Catalonia ranging around the Madres Massif north of Canigo and also in the Cadi Mountains, I was curious to know how a wolf ended up in a household in Fuengirola. At the next opportunity I put the question to Ramon.

'Via con Dios' he exclaimed 'Going with God' which probably meant he believed it was an act of God which brought the wolf to his door. I teased more details from him. Allowing for my poor Spanish and his faltering English I pieced together his description of how it must have been.

A Sunday night in late June. The household's three year old Labrador bitch was in heat and as a precaution Ramon had locked her in an outhouse for the night. The couple were awakened around three a.m. by a banging and crashing coming from their backyard area. From the bedroom window Ramon saw that the door to the outhouse where he kept his dog had been smashed from its hinges and that a huge wolf was mating with his Labrador bitch. The pair were 'in flagrante delicto' and because of wolf physiology they were locked together for quite some time. Maria urged Ramon to do something without specifying exactly what and Ramon simply chose the path of discretion and did nothing especially considering the size of the wolf which was massive. Also traditional Spanish folk tales about the existence of 'Werewolves' still circulated in some quarters and he was taking no chances. In the morning the wolf was gone, never to be seen again. After one month from the wolf incident Maria prevailed upon her husband to take Bonito, the dog to the Vet. After examination the bitch was pronounced to be pregnant. Since the gestation period for the wolf is much the same as the dog then it could be expected that Bonito would have her litter in nine to ten weeks. But all did not go as expected and Bonito suffered a sickly pregnancy and when seven weeks had elapsed the dog was so sick that a termination was mooted. However soon after that diagnosis Bonito's health improved and she was allowed to continue with the pregnancy. But there was another shock in store. It was found on examination that she was carrying only one embryo and it was large. When her time came for delivery it was thought best if she had her pup at the veterinary clinic. Complications aside Bonito give birth to a huge healthy male Pup that looked all wolf except for a light brown patch of Labrador hair across the saddle of his back. Bonito fawned on him which persuaded Ramon and Maria not to part with the wolf pup even though they were offered high prices for him. They were at a loss to decide upon a name until Ramon simply as a matter of routine called him Lobo (wolf) and it stuck. Outside the house he was referred to in awe as 'El Lobo.'

Lobo proved to be a handful of trouble for his owners. From incipient puppyhood he proved to be a ravening destructive force. Curtains and fabrics of any kind were targets for tearing and rendering. Prized household fixtures such as armchairs and a settee were ripped apart in a frenzy of plunder. A full length decorative steel security gate at the foot of the stairs was all that saved the bedrooms from similar mayhem. In despair the house proud couple were about to give him up when Lobo decided he'd had enough fun for the present and took to wrestling with his mother and later lying with her on the patio for a siesta. Whilst Maria was overjoyed at the prospect of refurbishing the house, Ramon fumed at the expense. Soon the old couple came to realise that El Lobo had his own agenda and nothing would deter him from it. This was to be his way for the rest of his life.

No doggy walks on the lead, no chasing balls thrown for his amusement, no training sessions along the pavement; only his own self- motivated behaviour. With this in mind one day when he was fourteen weeks old Lobo went walkabout and the remarkable thing about it was that he didn't put a paw wrong whether he was crossing the road or having a run along the beach, he did it in style. Dogs and people avoided contact with him like the plague and when he'd done his exercise he came home and lay on the cool pavement at the back of the house. Lobo ate whatever was laid before him whether it was dog meat or leftovers from the table. He was not an affectionate animal although he did respond a little to Maria when she stroked his head. Ramon by his own admission never touched him. "I am a leetle bit afraid of heem" he confided to me. The wonder is that they all lived together peacefully as a family. Lobo grew to an enormous size and in his prime he evidenced all the wild magnificence of a healthy wolf. This was how he was the first time I encountered him.

In seeking to make sense out of all I had heard about El Lobo I constructed an imaginary scenario for myself which might explain what had really happened.

It was a bitterly cold winter's day in the mountain border country. Fresh snow had fallen during the night and the wolf pack was closing in on a lone roe deer which was finding it heavy going through the soft snow. An icy wind from the mountains was scouring the bare terrain and lowering the temperature far below zero. The exhausted doe faltered and the wolves moved in for the kill. It was then that the hunters riding fast on their snow mobiles from downwind ambushed the wolf pack and began shooting. Caught by surprise the wolves abandoned their prey and tried to escape. The Alpha Male faced the hunters in a brave but futile attempt to cover the pack's getaway but was immediately cut down in a hail of bullets. Most of the rest suffered a similar fate. A young male of last year's litter stood paralysed with fear as he witnessed the Alpha Female, his mother, her back broken by heavy calibre shots struggling to reach him. She barked a command as she had done many times to him as a pup and exhorted him to run. He turned and fled for his life. Fragments of rock stung his sides from the blast of lead as he bolted away. He was the only survivor. Satisfied with their work the hunters began the grisly job of skinning the carcasses which would fetch high prices in the city markets of Barcelona and Madrid where cured wolf skin was a rare and fashionable commodity.

The young wolf ran all night stopping only twice to drink from snowmelt under bushes. He ran wolf like on his toes and effortlessly covered many miles before he took rest in the lee of some rocks on the southern slopes of the Sierra Nevada range. He was lonely for the safety and the comfort of his family, the wolf pack in which he'd been born. He slept fitfully crying and whimpering in his sleep as his dreams replayed the anguish of the massacre. In the days that followed he learned to hone the predatory skills he would need to survive. He lived on small game, rodents such as mice and rabbits and an occasional wildfowl. Twice he encountered other packs which he attempted to join but was chased off by the Alpha Males who would brook no foreigners. Eventually he accepted the role of the lone wolf who lived the life of an outcast surviving by means of his feral wits and the opportunities of chance. One night as he drifted much further south in his wandering, a stray wind bore a scent that he had never known before but which was so potent as to be irresistible to his masculine needs which were awakened with all their testosterone power. The scent led him down through housing developments where even the strong man smell could not deter him from his purpose. At last on tracing the dog bitch in heat he was so aroused by her calls that he forced his way into her shelter and mated with her. When they were done he suddenly became aware of frightening sounds closing all around him. He had never heard the sea before and it scared him now which together with the near proximity of humans was totally unnerving and he fled back to the safety of the mountains just as dawn was breaking never to venture that way again.

This waking dream of mine in which I speculated what probably happened endeared me to El Lobo who through an accident of birth was destined to live a civilised life even though he was much more of a wolf than dog. I was able to observe him many times as he sat his lonely vigil outside the family home looking wistfully towards the nearby foothills of the Sierra Morena which ultimately joined the Sierra Nevada mountain range. What questions I wondered coursed through that magnificent head? I asked Ramon one day if he had ever heard Lobo howl? "Never Senor, it would have scared me half to death" was his reply.

It was several months until I was again back in Fuengirola and able to renew my acquaintance with El Lobo. In the interim I had decided that I would attempt to speak to him. I have always believed in talking to the animals I have known in the firm conviction that they are able to understand the gist of what I am trying to communicate whether it is by tuning into the sentiments I express or picking up the images I project. I determined to give it a try. I chose an evening after he had done his customary constitutional lope along the beach and was resting on the patio outside. I moved as near to him as I dared and sat down on the ground facing him. I sensed an increase in alertness within him although he didn't move except to turn his head and stare directly at me. Ramon caught sight of me from the open door as he passed inside, smiled and called out "Be careful he don't eat you up!"

I addressed him in English because that is the language of my mind although aware that he would be accustomed chiefly to Spanish words. It was a communion of minds I was after reaching with him.

"Hello Wolf. I expect you have often wondered why you are destined to live here by the beach when your heart is longing for somewhere else. You know that your mother was a dog and that you are not like her because you are something different but you don't know what. I know what you are and that your father was a wolf who came down from the mountains you can see from your doorstep." As I said this he turned his gaze away from me and stared intently up at the hillsides to the west. I continued speaking to him. "Where you are looking is where your kind lives, they are wild wolves which dwell in the lonely places between the mountain passes to the north." When I said this I filled my mind with pictures to supplement my words. "You are one of them. They are your family and they need to hear from you because you are kin to them. Tell them you are here and they might answer you and then you will know what you truly are so that you can live your life in the contentment that you are a wolf."

As I arose to leave he turned once more to stare at me and if I am not mistaken there was a brightness in his eyes I hadn't seen there before. Several nights later as I lay sleepless in our apartment I distinctly heard a wolf howl. I got up and looked out the window. The sky was clear with a three quarters moon and a wolf was howling over and over again. It had to be El Lobo. He had got my message and I was glad to know finally that the species Canis Lupus was alive and well and thriving within him. One month later El Lobo disappeared. He could not be found anywhere. Ramon urged on by Maria made extensive inquiries regarding his whereabouts to no avail. It seems that after he had eaten one night he had decided to leave home. He was not there when Ramon closed the door for the night and there was no sign of him in the morning or ever again. Perhaps his howls had been answered. Perhaps the call of the wild had lured him away. Perhaps something came to seek him. No one knows but Ramon sleeps easy at nights now.

Printed in Great Britain
by Amazon